GUARDING ADELAIDE

A STEAMY, SMALL-TOWN PROTECTOR ROMANCE

GHOST LEGACY

PJ FIALA

I've had so many wonderful people come into my life and I want you all to know how much I appreciate it. From each and every reader who takes the time out of their day to read my stories and leave reviews, thank you.

My beautiful, smart and fun Road Queens, who play games with me, post fun memes, keep the conversation rolling and help me create these captivating characters, places, businesses and more. Thank you ladies for your ideas, support and love.

The following characters and places were created by:

Reader who named	Character/Place	Description
Amy Burkhart	**Ridley McCleskey**	Aide in Rafe's office
Charlene Burlison	**Robert Andrews**	Majority Leader
Karen Cranford LeBeau	**Senator Pierce Jackson**	Senator
Tracy Cruey	**Brooke Martin**	Rafe's sister
Pat Elliott	**Warren Elliott**	Red-haired man in the bar
Marie Evans	**Catalina**	Bowman Housekeeper
Stacy Hartley	**Jensen Gable**	Man who bombed the gym
Brenda Hojinski	**Bertrum Malachi**	Chief of Staff to Prime Minister of Yerezdan
Kristi Hombs Kopydlowski	**Chad Marshall**	Vice President Elect
	Ridley McCleskey	Aide in Rafe's office
	Daniel King	President Elect
Belinda Jackson Hercule	**Shanelle**	Bartender at Lawyer UP
	Brett Selisen	Aide in Rafe's office
	Brett Selisen	Aide in Rafe's office
Nathalie Juergensen	**Brent Martin**	Rafe's brother
Nancy Kehl	**Leesha**	Rafe's assistant
Jodi Krill	**Derek Mayes**	Alexandria Police Officer
Michelle Miller	**Clinton Miller**	Sketch Artist
Pamela Reveal	**Barrett Vickers**	Tate and Lara's son
Dana Zamora	**Lawyer Up to the Bar**	Bar in Washington D.C.
Debbie Zsidai	**Matt Holden**	Works at the DoD

Last but not least, thank you to my family for the love and sacrifices they have made and continue to make to help me achieve this dream, especially my husband and best friend, Gene. Words can never express how much you mean to me.

To our veterans and current serving members of our armed forces, police and fire departments, thank you ladies and gentlemen for your hard work and sacrifices; it's with gratitude and thankfulness that I mention you in this forward.

PJ Fiala

DESCRIPTION

GHOST: Government Hidden Ops Specialty Team. They eliminate the threat when no one else can.

She's following in her father's footsteps as a GHOST Operative.

He's the special counsel to the Secretary of Defense.

Their roles merge as a war breaks out that neither of them saw coming.

Adelaide Masters knew what she wanted from her earliest memories. Her cousins, Maya and Myles, along with the other children whose parents were special operatives with GHOST, were her constant companions growing up. Working under the watchful eyes of her family was the experience of a lifetime, but she's ready to set out on her own.

For fifteen years Rafe Martin has been living his dream as special counsel for the Secretary of Defense. It's a source of pride that he has been brought in on the most confidential assignments and what has brought him to this life-changing mission.

When Rafe's boss goes dark, and special operatives are brought in to secure him, Rafe finds resisting Adelaide's request for information at odds with his need to keep secrets. Now his secrets just may get Adelaide killed.

Guarding Adelaide is the fifth novel in the GHOST Legacy Romantic Suspense Series, although all books in the GHOST Legacy world can be read as a stand-alone. A steamy romantic story with a guaranteed happily ever after, it does have some strong language and exciting sexy times. Enjoy Rafe and Adelaide!

You're invited to join my readers club. I love staying in touch with readers and I try hard to make each newsletter both interesting and informative.

If you'd like to join me, click here and we'll get you signed up. Thank you so much. I hope you love Rafe and Adelaide!

If you're unable to click the link above, go here - https://www.pjfiala.com/subscribe/

GLOSSARY - GHOST LEGACY

Tate Vickers - Tate is the son of Gaige and Sophie Vickers. Their story is told in Defending Sophie. Tate is a recon specialist and runs the GHOST satellite office.

Aidyn Dunbar - Is the son of Bridget and Axel Dunbar. You can find their story is Defending Bridget. Aidyn's specialties are hand-to-hand.

Spencer Lawson - Spencer is the son of Wyatt and Yvette Lawson. You can read their story in Defending Yvette. Spencer specialize's in security, recon and recovery.

Henry Delany - Henry is the son of Hawk and Roxanne Delany. Their story is told is Defending Roxanne. His specialties are recon, recovery, and anything that requires size.

Adelaide Masters - Adelaide's parents are Josh and Isabella Masters. Their story is told in Defending Isabella. Adelaide served in the Army and is the team's medic.

Maya Sager - Maya served in the US Marine Corps.

Her parents are Dodge and Jax Sager. Their story is told in Finding His Jewel. Maya's specialty is recon and rescue.

Myles Sager - Myles served in the US Marine Corps. Myles and Maya are the twins of Dodge and Jax Sager. Myles is an explosives expert.

[illegible] now packed [illegible] briefcase and he [illegible] I was good. Not only not good, [illegible] would be the shit-show of all shit-shows. The president-elect was dirty. And, there was evidence. His stomach tightened like a fist before giving blood.

"Rafe, you are the most trustworthy person I know. I've counted on you for years now and I give you this informa-tion because [illegible] and you'll investigate it with the utmost thoroughness.

"You can count on me, sir." He said on autopilot. The beating of his heart drowned his words out to his own ears though.

"You're the only one I can count on. I've had GHOST called in. They'll be investigating Senator Jackson. I know he's dirty, he's admitted it. But, I need GHOST to dig into him fully. There are likely things he hasn't told me. I sent Gaige Vickers an encrypted file containing all I have. I've asked him not to open it unless something happens to me.

I've given him your name and contact information. I understand Adelaide Masters is the lead on this one. She's good. I've known her father for years and there isn't a person in the GHOST organization that isn't top notch."

He continued packing files into his briefcase as Rafe looked on.

"Yes, sir. I've been impressed with them for years now. They always manage to do what's needed."

"Okay. I'm stepping away for a few days to see if I can corroborate some of this information. You know how to reach me if you need me."

"Yes, sir."

His boss strode with purpose to the door. His posture always ramrod straight, but this was anything but a normal day and Rafe worried what their involvement and this investigation would mean in the future.

He stepped through the door to his own office and sat woodenly in the black leather chair behind the desk. In all his years climbing his way to the top, he'd never been tasked with something like this. Hell, he'd never considered something like this would ever come to pass. He wished his father could see him now. That old man was such a liar and a thief he'd never get over Rafe being considered trustworthy with information of this magnitude. What he wouldn't give to shove this in that old bastard's face.

He shook his head and abruptly stood. Thinking about his father never served him well. It always made him edgy and unfocused. Now more than ever, he needed focus.

He paced across the room to the door of his office and glanced across the outer office to his secretary. "Leesha,

I'm taking a bit of time to work out. I'll be back in the office in a couple of hours."

"Have a good workout, Mr. Martin. Did you see the Distible documents on your desk?"

"Ah, yes. I'll get to them when I get back."

He continued through the door of the outer office and down the hall. He shook his head, he hadn't seen the documents at all. Focus. He needed focus. Ducking through a private door to a back hallway, he left the building without notice to anyone else. His boss had this door put in years ago. The funniest thing was no one ever asked or seemed to notice it. Then again, if a stranger to this office building came into this hallway, it looked like a hall of doors, so what was one more?

Ducking into the parking lot, he jumped into his Range Rover with ease and navigated the staff parking lot of the building with little effort. Entering Washington traffic, he merged into the string of cars and trucks like anyone else. But he wasn't anyone else. He had a secret that was going to blow this town apart.

Shaking off his paranoia, he navigated traffic until he turned into the parking lot of the gym he preferred over the one at the DoD building. He hated being asked questions at the gym there. Here, he was just Rafe Martin, a guy who worked out.

Preferring a long swim today, he quickly donned his swim trunks and swim shoes, locked his locker and headed to the pool. At two in the afternoon, it was empty, which was his preference. Striding to the deep end of the pool he jumped in. Beginning his laps, he worked to remove all negative thoughts from his mind. He abused his body with hard laps, gasping for air as his lungs burned with the lack of it. His shoulders began to weaken as he finished his twentieth lap and since his mind was still in a state of what-the-fuck, he did another five.

Upon exiting the pool, he forced his weakened legs to carry him to the locker room. A balding man startled as Rafe entered the locker room. The man quickly dropped his hands and hurried toward the door. Rafe crept toward his locker and found the lock had deep gashes on it as if someone had tried to pry it open.

He spun around and sprinted toward the door to find the man he'd seen leaving just moments before. Just as he entered the gym's main floor, he saw the man look back at him. An explosion erupted from behind him. Chaos, panic, and terror filled the building as the patrons began screaming and running blind. Rafe was engulfed in people, smoke, and debris before he could get to the door to stop him.

His ringing ears filled with screams and crying as the dust rose. Coughing, he helped a woman who had fallen and cut her knees on broken glass. She tried standing, but her wobbly legs wouldn't move her fast enough, so Rafe easily picked her up and took her to the front doors, where throngs of people now huddled as staff tried encouraging them to the back of the parking lot.

Ignoring the gym staff, Rafe ducked back into the building and took the back way to the pool area. The water now flooding the floor suggested the pool area had been hit. A young woman, likely in her early twenties, tried stopping his progress. "I'm sorry sir, you'll need to go outside with the others."

Rafe stared into her eyes. As much as either of them could with the dust still swirling. "I'm military police, here to work out."

Her eyes widened then squinted with the air quality so poor. Deciding not to bother further, she shrugged and said, "Suit yourself." She disappeared around a corner and Rafe eased his way into the locker room that led to the pool.

2

___

[illegible] room, [illegible] living room. It [illegible] aesthetics of the old [illegible], they occupied as their home, office, and garage, HOG would shine through. Tate's mom, Sophie, and Henry's mom, Roxanne, had done a fabulous job of designing the space. It was the perfect blend of old and new.

Sitting [illegible] Tate [illegible] as her teammates entered the room one by one. First Myles, directly behind her, sat to her right. Henry entered next, and sat across from her, he smelled like a horse. Spencer entered next, freshly showered and looking like he was heading out on a date with Kenna. Maya came last, eating an apple.

Maya sat at the end of the table. Her nose wrinkled and her eyes landed on each of them one by one. "We need to have a rule that you need to shower before coming to a meeting and sitting in a glass room."

Adelaide chuckled and stared at her cousin. Maya's

pretty face lit up, a cocky smile slid across her lips. "It smells like horses in here."

Addy burst out laughing and the entire room turned toward Henry. "I was called to an emergency meeting, so I dropped everything and ran over. Deal with it."

Addy shook her head. "Not entirely true."

Henry shrugged one beefy shoulder. "I'm getting married and we were excited to tell you all. But now Ev is sitting in the kitchen by herself while I'm in here."

Spencer grinned. "Congrats. Kenna and Lara are in the kitchen with Everleigh. They were mixing up drinks when I left."

Tate tapped his forefinger on the table. "Okay. Listen up. First of all, Maya, you've smelled much worse before."

Maya's brows bunched together. "Gee, thanks."

"Second of all, I changed the grossest diaper ever today and this room smells like a flower garden compared to that. Unless you want some diaper duty of your own, zip it."

Maya shook her head and held her hands, apple and all, out in front of her. "No. Thank. You."

Addy laughed. "I second Maya."

"Okay. Kidding aside, we've got an issue. I received a call from my dad. He received a call from Casper. From what they've managed to deduce, Wade Evans, the Secretary of Defense, received some information from a Senator Pierce Jackson with damning information about our newly elected president, Daniel King. Casper refused to say more than that but said they both may have to go dark if some of this information is fact."

Addy sat back in her chair and her brows furrowed. Casper had been giving them missions long before she was born. All any of them knew about him was that he worked for the Department of Defense. The rest was a mystery. Over the years, GHOST, her father's generation, had tried figuring out who Casper was, but he was good at secrecy. He'd been bigger than life in her mind forever. He was this mystical creature who was using them to right wrongs of the world. She loved that they didn't know who he was. But the fact he might be in trouble, that was scary.

"That's not good." She mumbled.

Tate nodded. "Right. That's what we all feel. I need three operatives to go to Washington and ferret out Senator Jackson. See if you can get him to talk. If you can't, you'll need to find a way to figure out what he told Casper that has him worried."

Addy surged forward in her chair. "I'll go."

Myles quickly said, "Me too."

Tate nodded at them, then turned to Henry. "We're using your grandparents' home as our home base in Washington. Do you want to be there too?"

Henry nodded. "Of course."

"Good, you know the area better than anyone here. And, from what I'm told, the housekeeper, Catalina, will be excited to see you."

Henry's cheeks turned a deep pink. Addy grinned. "Oh, is there a story there?"

Henry swallowed. "No. But she thinks I'm cute. And, she's my mom's age, so that's the gist of it."

Myles burst out laughing. "Is she blind?"

Henry grinned. "She has twenty-twenty vision. So, when she sees you, it'll be hard for her not to grimace."

Myles laughed and lifted his middle finger.

Tate chuckled slightly but brought the conversation

back to the task, or mission, at hand. "So you three need to pack. Gavin will be here with the plane in three hours. The Bowman home is well equipped, so you won't need little necessities, just clothes, laptops, equipment. I'll get the equipment bags ready while you pack. Addy, I'd like you in charge of this mission."

"Thank you. I accept."

Maya stood. "I can help with the equipment."

"Great. Thank you everyone. Addy, Myles, and Henry, I have the files we got from headquarters uploaded to the server. You can read up on the flight to Washington."

She had goose bumps on her arms. Excited didn't half describe how she felt. Maya joined her in her room. "You're practically beaming."

Reaching to the back of her closet, she pulled her suitcase out and laid it on her bed, next to her cousin.

"I'm so ready for this mission. I've been going stir-crazy here."

"Yeah. Me too, but I hate Washington."

Pulling her top drawer open she pulled out her undergarments. "I've only been once, but I'm dying to see the Bowman home."

Maya laughed. "My mom said it was amazing."

Addy dropped her clothing on the bed next to her suitcase and began refolding it to fit in packing cubes before arranging them in her suitcase. She looked up at Maya, "I know I don't need to remind you, but I'm going to anyway. If anything happens to me..."

"Stop. I know. You've told me where you keep everything. I'll make sure Uncle Josh and Aunt Isi are okay."

"And...?"

Maya huffed out a breath. "And, I'll plant a tree for you at headquarters next to Jake and Grandpa's."

Addy nodded and let out a breath to vanquish the negative feelings that evoked. But, there was always a possibility that things could go wrong. Their family knew it more than others. Their grandfather, Richard Masters, had been killed on a mission as well as their Uncle Jake Masters. It was a reality. But a reality they accepted.

nearly turned
ntly occupied.
ing lot and his vehicle, from his
office window. He liked keeping an eye on all things.

Exiting his vehicle, he hit the lock button on his key fob and pocketed his keys. His mind snapped as it ran through the scenario of today. He'd memorized that man. The balding man who was in the locker room. He'd have one of his aides upload his database, run it through a recognition program, first thing. His memory was great, nearly ninety percent recall, but there was no reason to test that right now.

Opening his laptop on his desk, he emailed the sketch artist they had on staff at the DoD, to set up an appointment as soon as possible. His phone buzzed and he picked it up automatically, Leesha was gone for the day.

"Martin."

"Mr. Martin, my name is Adelaide Masters. I work for GHOST. I was given your contact information as our on-the-ground contact in Washington."

"Yes, Ms. Masters. How can I help you?"

"You can start by calling me Adelaide, or Addy. That's what my friends call me. I'm looking for any insight you might have on the whereabouts of Senator Jackson."

Rafe pulled open his bottom right-hand drawer, unlocked the false side, and pulled out a file. Laying it neatly on his desk, he flipped it open and scanned the top page. He then entered an access code into the secure section of the private server Casper had inside the DoD server.

"As of three hours ago, Senator Jackson was in person at a Senate council meeting. He lost his re-election campaign and has been rattling cages about broken promises and being stabbed in the back."

"Is he being followed?"

"Somewhat."

"How do you somewhat, follow someone?"

"Suffice it to say, we have people placed in strategic places that can offer us information."

"Fair enough. So this was three hours ago. Any mention of his whereabouts now?"

"Not here, but I can make a couple of calls. Are you in Washington?"

"Yes, we've recently arrived at the Bowman home and have set up operations here. Our next step is to locate Senator Jackson and see if we can get him to talk to us."

"I'll call you back in a few minutes."

"Thank you."

The line went dead and he sat for a moment and stared at his phone. It was game on now. GHOST was in place. His life, all of their lives were likely to change tenfold within a day or two. Never in his wildest dreams did he think he'd be in this position.

He dialed up one of his contacts. "Yeah."

"I need to know the whereabouts of Senator Jackson."

"On it."

A click then silence on the other end.

His phone rang again as he held it. "Martin."

"Casper. What the hell happened at the gym today?"

"Someone set off a bomb. It was small and only damaged the pool area, part of the locker room and the blast blew down the hallway to the main area, creating mass chaos and damage."

"Was it directed at you?"

"I'm not sure. No one would have known I was going to the gym today. It was impromptu."

"But you didn't report it."

"I didn't want to tip my hand. I spoke to police just like any other gym goer. GHOST is in place now so I'll let them in on this as soon as the police department gets back to me. I saw a man leaving the locker room and my locker had been carved up as if someone was trying to get inside. I have an email in to the sketch artist here. As soon as I have a graphic, I'll run it through and see if I can figure out who he is and why he's targeting me - if he was, or the gym if he wasn't."

"Does anyone know you're working with me?"

"No sir. If they've figured it out, it didn't come from me."

He heard Casper take a deep breath and let it out slowly. "Keep me informed."

"Yes sir. But, if no one knows we're working together, I don't see why they'd target me to get to you."

The line went dead before an answer was given. He abruptly stood and paced to the window. His vehicle sat where he had parked it. The parking spots on either side were vacant. The sun was beginning to set and his mind wandered to the activities of today.

His phone rang once again and he wondered when he'd ever get a half hour of peace and quiet to actually get work done. Snatching it from his desk he kept his voice even.

"Martin."

"Senator Jackson is at a bar called Lawyer Up To The Bar."

"Is he alone?"

"He went in alone. He's now pointing fingers and accusing people of deserting him."

"Keep me apprised if it goes off the rails."

"Roger."

Packing his laptop into his leather carry case, locking his desk drawers, and perusing the office for anything out of place, Rafe hefted his laptop case over his shoulder and exited his office, locking the door on the way out.

Janitorial staff were in the halls, most of the building's occupants now gone for the day. He inhaled a breath of fresh air on his way to his vehicle, and mentally prepared for the coming events.

After locking his car doors, he tapped the Bluetooth button on his steering wheel and said, "Call Adelaide Masters."

The robotic voice replied. "Calling Adelaide Masters."

The phone rang only twice. "Masters."

"Hello, Adelaide, it's Rafe Martin. Senator Jackson is at Lawyer Up To The Bar, a little place on Downey Street, just off of U Street. Many of the congressional folks hang out there."

"Got it. We'll head over now."

"I understand he's causing trouble and accusing

members of congress of not supporting his campaign. He may get himself kicked out before you get there."

He heard a light chuckle and imagined her smile. All he'd seen so far were head shots in the file Casper kept. She was a beautiful woman. He wondered how she managed a love life when she worked for a covert organization such as GHOST. It was similar in many ways to his job. He'd never found the right woman who could handle the weird hours and last-minute change of plans. There was a time he'd been through a string of girlfriends hoping one of them would manage to deal with his life. But, in the end none of them could and he got tired of the upheaval when they ultimately dumped him. He was now on his own.

4

[illegible] alone. She [illegible] meeting in five

[illegible]

"Roger."

Her teammates replied. She pulled open the door and schooled her features when the odor of old beer, cigar smoke, and body odor assaulted her. Another din of [illegible] Washington had laws [illegible] smoking in public places order, yet here were all the congressional law makers doing what they wanted regardless. These assholes would have other bar owners fined for allowing this. Maya was right about hating Washington. It was a cesspool of the worst kind.

She spotted Senator Jackson right away. Not because he was so handsome. Far from it. He was a hundred pounds overweight. Balding. The hair he did have needed to be cut six months ago. He had a half-assed comb-over which literally consisted of about ten hairs. His clothes fit sloppily, his posture was nonexistent. All in all, what else could this frump do for a living except this?

He stood in the middle of the floor, pointing his pudgy forefinger at another man who looked him in the eye and stared him down as Senator Jackson spewed.

"You promised if I voted for your mother-fucking farm-aid bill you'd stump for me and advertise with me. When the time to pay up came along, you were hard to fucking find."

The younger gentleman simply shrugged a shoulder and took a drink from his bottle of beer.

Myles and Henry entered the bar from the back and ambled closer to the melee to hear Senator Jackson expel profanities and accusations. The nod she gave them was so slight you'd have to be looking to see it.

The younger man tired of Senator Jackson's mudslinging and walked away, missing the swing Senator Jackson flailed at him.

Henry stepped in front of Senator Jackson and softly said, "Can I buy you a drink. It seems as though you've had a hard time of it and could use one."

"Yeah. Yeah. Hard time. Fuckers hung me out to dry."

Addy neared the bar where there were three empty stools and plopped down on the farthest one to the left. Henry steered Senator Jackson to the middle stool, next to her and planted himself on the other. Myles stood to the end of the bar, watching for signs of danger. Maybe retaliation for the senator's harsh words this evening. As the drinks flowed, tempers seemed to shorten.

Senator Jackson tapped his fingers on top of the bar. "Bartender!" He bellowed. "Give me a beer."

The woman behind the bar glanced at him. Her lips turned down at the corners and her wary, or maybe weary eyes looked into Addy's. Addy grinned slightly and nodded in commiseration and the woman behind the bar turned and pulled a bottle of beer from the bank of coolers behind her.

Opening the bottle, she set it down neatly on a coaster with the bar's name printed in red around it. Henry spoke up. "This is on me. I'll take a Coors and get the little lady what she wants."

The bartender stepped in front of Addy. "What'll you have hon?"

"I'll have a Coors too. Thank you." She smiled brightly, knowing this woman was likely in need of someone less surly and more friendly by this point.

She returned Addy's smile, set the beers on the bar, neatly in the middle of the coasters and Henry threw money on the bar. "Get yourself something too."

The woman bit her bottom lip and hesitated. Addy encouraged her. "If you can't drink behind the bar, get a soda or something. But you need to keep yourself hydrated."

The grateful bartender nodded and pulled a can of soda from the cooler.

Senator Jackson huffed out a breath. "Thanks for the drink. What're you after?"

Henry shook his head. "I'm not after anything. It simply looked like you needed a break. When I came in it looked like you against the entire bar."

Addy picked up her beer bottle and held it up toward Henry. "Thank you."

"You're welcome."

Senator Jackson turned to her then, "I haven't seen you here before."

"No, I'm from out of town. My friend said she and her

husband visited here last year and it was worth checking out."

"It's kind of a shithole." The senator responded. "But, we like it here because we're largely left alone. Out on U Street, people are always asking us to vote for this bill or help with that bill or whatever the new need is for the day. Sometimes it's nice to come here and not be hounded."

Addy nodded. "I can see that. But it sure looked like you weren't having any fun a bit ago."

"No. They're all greedy sons-a-bitches and don't follow through on their promises."

"I'm sorry. That sucks."

"It sure as shit does." He took a long pull off his beer.

"What did they not follow through on?" She smiled at him, hoping he'd continue to chat.

"They were supposed to stump for me and help me with my re-election. But not one of them did. It's all King's fault."

"Who's King?"

He turned his head, his flabby cheeks moving at weird angles when he did. "Daniel King. As in president-elect, Daniel King."

"Oh." She straightened. "He told them not to help you?"

A round shoulder hitched up and fell. "Not in so many words. But, by alliance only."

"I don't understand." She cocked her head to the left and stared at him.

He stared at her for a moment, then took another pull off his beer. "It doesn't matter."

"Did you have a fight with him?"

"Sort of. It's over now." His voice changed and so did his demeanor. He was a defeated man.

"Is there anything I can do?"

He laughed then. A short bark of laughter before he locked eyes with her in the mirror behind the bar. "Not unless you have a time machine and can go back to about eight years ago. My whole life would be completely different if you could. And some people would still be alive."

Henry responded to the cryptic comment. "Boy, I've been there." He looked past Senator Jackson to her. "Do you have a time machine?"

"'Fraid not." She chuckled.

The front door opened and a tall thin man with reddish hair strode into the bar. His eyes scanned the people inside before he took a seat at the curve of the bar near the door.

Senator Jackson shifted on his barstool and muttered something, but she couldn't hear what he said.

"I'm sorry, I didn't hear you."

The senator squirmed on his stool and stared at the end of the bar. "One of these assholes in here likely told him I was here." He said softly.

"Who is that?" she questioned.

The senator shrugged. "It doesn't matter."

Addy sipped her beer but made sure she made eye contact with Myles. He nodded and pulled his phone out of his pocket.

Senator Jackson's phone buzzed in his pocket, but he ignored it.

"Aren't you going to answer your phone?"

"No."

He chugged the remainder of his beer and tapped the bottom of his bottle on the bar. The bartender glanced at her, as if she were seeking permission. She smiled sweetly and nodded.

The bartender's shoulders drooped before she turned and pulled another beer from the cooler and set it in front of the senator.

He dropped money on the bar and pointed with his thumbs to Henry and her. "Get my friends one too."

Addy smiled. "Thank you."

The bartender pulled two more beers from the cooler and set them on the bar. The senator's beefy hand pushed his money to the edge. The bartender grabbed the money, strode to the cash register and brought back change, barely stopping to make sure it all landed on the bar. She breezily scooted to the end of the bar and took the drink order of the reddish-haired man.

The senator's phone rang again and he inhaled a deep breath and let it out in a huff. Squirming on the stool to pull his phone from his trouser pockets, he tapped the icon. "Yeah."

Between the music and the talking, it was impossible to hear the other end of the conversation, but his body language told her it wasn't a good call.

"I'm aware. He's sitting right where I can see him."

5

[illegible] home. [illegible] after his [illegible] neighborhood he'd waited for [illegible] Arlington Heights. Elite, close to the Pentagon and secure. He'd spent most of his life in barracks and shitty apartments enough to know that as soon as he could afford a home, it would be here. He'd hired an interior designer to decorate before he moved in. She'd captured him [illegible] further.

All warm tones and leather furniture, he'd once been told by a female friend that it was the perfect man cave. And, it was. It was perfect for him.

He crossed the foyer into the spacious living room, his eyes always landing on the floor-to-ceiling brick fireplace nestled between mahogany built-in shelves. On the shelves were photographs of his sister, Brooke, who was two years younger, and his brother, Brent, who was four years younger. Both of them lived far away from their parents as well. But that also meant, they didn't see each other as often as he'd like.

Brooke was a photographer, now taking photos of cover models for books and enjoying every minute of it. And Brent was working for a large corporation in the design and development area. Rafe was the only one who entered the military.

Stepping into his office, he tucked his briefcase under the desk. He then moved to his bedroom and pulled off his suit jacket, and neatly hung it in the closet in the space it held this morning.

He quickly changed into dark blue sweatpants and a white t-shirt. Letting out a sigh of relief, he made his way to the kitchen and opened the refrigerator. He'd planned on making spaghetti tonight, all the ingredients waiting for him on the second shelf. Laying his phone on the counter, he popped open his music app, tapped his playlist, and began cutting up a green pepper as music filled his house.

He browned his ground beef, added the peppers and onions, and set the lid on the pan to let the flavors fuse when his phone rang.

Stifling his irritation, he tapped the answer icon. "Rafe Martin."

"Mr. Martin, this is Clinton Miller, the sketch artist at the DoD. I received your email. When would you like to meet?"

"Is tonight out of the question?"

"No sir. I can meet you at the office."

Rafe looked down at his clothing, inhaled the aroma of his dinner, and his shoulders slumped. "How about this. I'm just ready to eat dinner and I'm dressed in casual attire. We can meet at the office as long as we don't need to dress up."

Clinton laughed. "I'm so on board with that. I just got

home myself and saw your email. Casual sounds perfect."

"I'll be there in an hour."

"I'll be there as well. Do you know where my office is?"

Rafe stirred his sauce. "I do. I'll see you soon."

The line went dead, his music began filtering through the built-in speakers around his home once again, and he poured himself a glass of wine. Yes, he was going back to work, but you can't eat spaghetti without wine. One glass would be fine and he'd call a driver. All good.

After finishing his dinner, Rafe texted a car service, donned his tennis shoes, pocketed his wallet, his phone and his keys, and waited for the car.

His phone buzzed in his pocket. One glance and he noted his car was out front. He stepped out into the warm evening air, strode to the car, and slid easily into the backseat. "The Pentagon, please."

Rafe watched the lights of the city as they drove by. He thought back to the day's events, he could still see the man leaving the locker room. His facial features were as clear as this taxi driver's, though he tried not looking at the driver too much, he didn't need to test his memory.

The car stopped in front of the main entrance, he paid on his app. "Please come back here in an hour."

"Yes, sir. I'll be right here."

Rafe left a large tip to ensure he would and slid out of the backseat with ease.

He stepped to the security desk, showed his ID, scanned himself in and trooped down the hall to Clinton Miller's office.

The door opened before he arrived, a younger man, thin with sharp features stepped into the hall and held his hand out in greeting.

"Hello, Mr. Martin, Clinton Miller."

"Hello, Mr. Miller."

They stepped into the office, which was lit by the florescent lights used all over government buildings, though some of that had changed to more energy efficient bulbs. This was a huge building and it would take time to get to them all.

"Please sit down, Mr. Martin."

"You may as well call me Rafe."

Clinton nodded and replied. "You should call me Clint."

He pulled a sketch pad from a closet and laid it on the desktop. Pulling open drawers, he set pencils next to the pad and sat at his desk. A portable easel was pulled from a bottom desk drawer. As Clint opened it up and arranged it, he said, "I'm sorry I'm not ready. I just arrived myself."

"No problem. Take your time."

Clint arranged his sketch pad on the easel, pulled a stool toward the desk and replaced his chair with it, then sat atop it with a flourish. "Okay, now let's start."

Rafe related his memory of the man's face. His eyes, the color of them, his cheeks, his chin, the stubble and the mole near the left eye. He slowly and diligently described each feature as his eye saw it. Clint didn't interrupt him, but his pencil moved across the sketch pad as if in a fever, the soft brushing sound was mesmerizing in its fluidity.

After nearly forty-five minutes, Clint turned the easel toward him, "Take a look at this and tell me what's off."

"His brows were a bit bushier. He had lines under his eyes."

Clint moved his pencil across the man's face and turned it toward him again.

"Perfect. That's the man I saw."

6

"I'm being followed."

"I don't understand."

"It doesn't matter." He polished off the remainder of his beer and stood.

"Will you be alright?"

He mumbled something under his breath and Addy glanced at Henry. He nodded and began following the senator to the back door.

She still had a full beer, the one the senator purchased, sitting on the bar untouched and she nodded to the bartender. "Not sure if you want it, but I haven't touched it. I've got to go."

The bartender stopped in front of her and pulled the bottle off the bar and dumped it in a garbage can. She stared at Addy for a moment. "What's up with you and the senator?"

"Nothing. I came to see the place, saw him having some troubles, and wanted to help."

She bit her bottom lip, her dark hair pulled back into a ponytail at the top of her head. "I don't buy it."

Addy shrugged. "So, who's the redhead at the end of the bar?"

The bartender turned her head, stared briefly at the man, who was watching them closely then looked her in the eyes again.

"I think he works for the president-elect. I've seen them together, though not for a while now. Once Senator King started campaigning, he stopped coming in. But, that man is known in this area as a snitch or an informant."

"For president-elect King?"

"And others."

"Do you know who likely just called Senator Jackson?"

The bartender leaned forward, a smile crawled across her face. "And you want to know, why?"

Addy grinned and shrugged a shoulder. "I think he might be in trouble."

"No shit." She picked up a bar rag and swiped across the top of the bar in front of where the senator and Henry had sat, then looked her way again.

"What does that mean? Is it common knowledge that the senator is in trouble?"

"Let's just say he's been poking a stick at all the bears these days. He's so bitter about losing his senate seat and he's blaming everyone for not helping him. When someone yells too loudly, people do things to shut them up. I've seen it happen time and again."

"As in what kind of things?"

"Their bills are suddenly not pushed through. They

lost staff members to other staff members. They don't get reelected. And some of them get un-alived."

"As in who got un-alived?"

The bartender took a deep breath and shrugged her shoulders. "I'll just say, if you look up the murders in this area over the past two years, you'll see a very long list. Granted this town is a shithole of epic proportions. But, have you noticed that most of these murders are nothing more than a quick mention on the evening news and then nothing is spoken of again. The family members quietly move away. No one screams and yells that justice isn't being done here. Nothing. People are just dead and no one is held accountable."

"Why do you stay here?"

She shook her head and looked down at the bar. When she raised her head, her eyes were glistening and her nose had a pinkish color to it. "I barely make enough money here to pay my rent, let alone be able to afford to move. I would if I could. Believe me."

"Shanelle, are you having trouble or telling secrets?"

She looked up to see the red-haired man from the end of the bar had joined them. Addy looked at him, up close he had small blue eyes, and his lashes were nearly invisible. "It's just girl talk."

Shanelle stiffened and wiped the bar in front of her. The red-haired man watched Shanelle for a moment, then walked toward the back door that Henry and the senator had gone through.

Addy pulled a card from her pocket, it was a simple business card they each had with basic information on it. GHOST used a fictitious name on the card, GV Security. Her first name and a phone number that ran through the GHOST computers first and then to her. Every call was recorded and mapped. They only used them sparingly. "If you ever need help, or feel as though you are in trouble, please call me."

Shanelle looked at the card, then into her eyes. "I figured you were more than just a tourist."

Addy winked at her. "Remember, if you need help, call me."

Addy turned to see Myles watching them. She was eager to see if Henry had any luck with the senator. Weaving through the crowd, which had grown a bit since they'd arrived an hour ago, she had to school her features to not grimace as the leaches that hung out here bumped into her. Stepping out the back door she finally took a full breath.

Myles exited behind her. "What a shithole."

"The whole town is."

"Right." Myles stepped to the edge of the property and looked down the alleyway behind the building. "Henry, where are you?"

A tapping sound came over the comm unit before Henry's voice. "I'm in the truck."

"Roger."

She ambled along the alley with Myles alongside. Both of them watched every nook and cranny along the way. It was fairly dark and the entrances to some of the places didn't have a light over the door, making it inky black.

Stepping onto U Street the activity was in direct opposition to the quietness of the alley. People whizzed past on rented scooters and e-bikes. Tourists walked along the sidewalk looking in every direction except where they were going.

Arriving at the truck, she hopped into the passenger

seat. Myles climbed in behind her. Henry turned to them, "The senator called a car and took off without saying much. He did manage to mumble that his number is up. And, he said, "'Good thing Wade knows.'"

"Who's Wade?" She asked.

"I have a call in to Tate to find out if he knows."

[illegible] in the [illegible] before all the [illegible]. Now that [illegible] he had a hard time finding a few minutes of peace between phone calls. His boss was out for the foreseeable future and he had a lot of interference to run.

Opening his laptop, the first thing that caught his attention was a search being performed on his boss. He recalled the number of times his name [illegible]. Times his name had been typed in. Location pins where he was located. Sensitive information for just anyone to find.

The burning in his stomach felt like a gut punch. Picking up his cell phone he dialed his boss's phone number.

"What do you need, Rafe?"

"I just opened my laptop to see someone searching your name. All of our geotags are lit up like a Christmas tree. Even your location. You need to power down and go dark."

"Doing it now. You have my burner number?"

"Yes. Check in twice a day."

"Roger."

He hung up and added tags of his own on the IP address the searches were coming from. All of them centered around three locations. Washington. Indiana. Kentucky.

Slamming the lid on his laptop, he packed it all back up and slung his case over his shoulder and he hustled from his office and the building. It would take him less than twenty minutes to arrive at the Washington address. Traffic considered. It was still early by political standards.

He tapped the Bluetooth in his vehicle. "Call Leesha."

"Calling Leesha." Came the robotic voice.

The phone rang twice before her voicemail picked up. As soon as the beep sounded, he left his message. "Leesha, I won't be in for a while. I had to run over to Washington on business. Please clear my calendar for the day. I'll let you know when I'll be back."

Tapping the end call button, he turned up the street where the pin on the map glowed bright red. The driveways in this part of town were in the back, so he parked on the street in front of the house. It was palatial and surrounded by large hedges and perfect landscaping. He knew where he was.

Taking a deep breath, he exited his vehicle and stalked up the sidewalk that led to the red front door. The bright flowers that bloomed up the walkway made for a pleasant walk. It created a happy feeling before guests arrived.

He alighted the three large steps to the covered landing. Pushing the doorbell, he heard the soft piano notes of Mozart's Piano Sonata No. 11 in A major. He'd studied classical music for a couple of semesters, just enough that he could speak about it at high-class functions. It wasn't necessarily his type of music, but he recognized it.

The door opened and a woman in her early forties appeared with a smile on her face.

"Hello. How may I help you?"

"I'm here to see Adelaide Masters and company."

"Yes. Who may I say is here?"

"Rafe Martin."

"Yes, Mr. Martin. Please come in."

He stepped into the foyer of the home, which was larger than most people's living rooms. It was open and inviting. The marble floor gleamed in the light of the chandelier above. The large circular staircase hugged the wall to the right and gracefully widened at the bottom.

"Come into the living room please and I'll let Ms. Masters know you're here."

She led him to the left where a large room carpeted in white, with lighter toned furniture sat in perfect groupings for private chats. The stone fireplace flowed to the ceiling, much like his own. He halted before stepping onto the pristine white carpet, wondering if he should take his shoes off. The woman nodded. "It's alright. Please make yourself comfortable."

She left quietly, and he sat in a chair facing the staircase across the foyer and next to the fireplace.

Within a few minutes a gorgeous woman of Hispanic descent, with long dark hair descended the staircase. Though she wore jeans and a dark gray t-shirt, she looked like a goddess. Her movements were fluid. She practically floated.

He stood and watched her. The instant their eyes met he felt it. Something similar to an electrical current sizzled down his spine. The hairs at the nape of his neck prickled.

She floated across the foyer, her shoes barely making a sound. The instant she stopped in front of him, her hand held out in greeting, she said, "Hello, Rafe. I'm Adelaide Masters. Or Addy if you prefer."

He steadied himself and held his hand out to hers. The instant their palms touched, he wrapped his fingers around her petite hand. "It's nice to meet you."

She smiled and held her hand out to his chair indicating he sit. She took the chair next to his. "We didn't know you were coming."

Didn't she feel something?

"I didn't intend on coming until I saw that you were tracking Wade Evans."

Her facial expression didn't change. Note to self - don't play cards with Adelaide Masters.

"How do you know who we're tracking?"

"There are certain people it's my responsibility to take care of and Mr. Evans is one of them. He's also my boss."

She nodded. "Yes, I see the connection now. He's the Secretary of Defense and you are his Special Counsel."

"Yes."

She nodded. "And our search for Mr. Evans triggered your system?"

"Yes." He leaned slightly forward. "Now I need to ask why you're trying to locate Mr. Evans."

She smiled. He was left speechless for just a moment as he took in her beauty. She was radiant. But he also knew she was lethal. Maybe that was the attraction. She was someone similar to him.

"We have guests." A large man entered the room with a grin on his face.

"Yes, Mr. Delany, I'm Rafe Martin."

His brows rose into his dark hair and his grin widened. "You've been looking into us."

"It's my job."

"You can call me Henry." He neared and held his hand out. His handshake was firm and professional.

"Then, please call me Rafe."

Henry sat on the sofa across from him. He made the furniture look small. He was built like his father. "It must feel good to be back in your grandparents' home after all this time."

Henry shrugged one beefy shoulder. "To be honest, we came here as children, but my grandparents were murdered before I was born. So, it doesn't hold the type of childhood memories for me that it does for my mother. For us, it was a visit to see that all was well. Maybe my uncles and cousins would come also, but that was sporadic. We're located all over the country."

"I understand."

Footsteps and chattering filtered into the room, then a tall dark-haired man of Hispanic descent entered the room. He resembled Addy in some ways. Same nose and chin. The woman who had opened the door followed him with a tray filled with glasses and a pitcher of lemonade.

"Hello, Rafe, I'm Myles Sager. It's nice to meet you."

He shook hands, once again impressed by this group.

Myles sat on the sofa opposite Henry. "Catalina made us lemonade. She'll be disappointed if we don't drink it."

Henry chuckled and began pouring glasses for each of them.

Addy took her glass from Henry. "Rafe came here because he knows we were looking into Wade Evans. Wade is his boss."

Myles nodded and crossed his left ankle over his right knee.

"We weren't clued in on the connection."

Rafe watched them all. They weren't covertly glancing at each other, but he already knew Addy was careful with her facial expressions. "I need to know why you were searching for Mr. Evans."

8

A[illegible] He carried himself with [illegible] health and proper [illegible] He had a confidence that thrilled her. And, when their hands touched, she felt a current run up her arm.

Henry nodded. "Last night we met up with Senator Jackson, as you know. Or, at least you notified us of his location. A red-headed man entered the bar as we spoke with him [illegible] Then he got a phone call that sent him out of the bar. I followed him and he mumbled something about Wade. I believe he said, "At least Wade knows." We began searching for Wades in Washington, focusing on those associated in high places."

Rafe nodded and she stared. His profile was classic. His skin was flawless. Though he wore a suit jacket, the muscles in his arms filled his jacket out perfectly.

"Based on your search and ability to locate his where-abouts, I've asked him to go dark."

Addy tilted her head. "Is he in trouble?"

"I don't know."

"Why would he need to go dark just because we searched for him?"

He turned and locked eyes with her. She felt a thrill as she stared into his eyes. Dark brown, clear, and framed by a thick set of lashes. But, mostly, they didn't look away from her. "The geo pins I have on Mr. Evans are colored. Your search is one color. But there was another color also searching for him last night. That one I couldn't pinpoint. As soon as they found him, they jumped out before my software could hold the position. Which worries me they may have an idea that I have geo pins. Or, they had a bad connection. Or, it could be any number of reasons, but others are looking for him."

Myles leaned forward, placing his elbows on his knees. "Any idea who might be trying to locate him?"

"No. Do you?"

"Not yet. Any idea where the senator is now?"

Rafe pulled his phone from his trouser pocket and tapped a few times. His fingers were strong and sure as he texted.

"I'll know in a few minutes."

Addy watched him closely. "What about Casper? Has he also gone dark?"

Rafe moved deliberately. He sat straight and once again, looked her in the eye. "I believe he has also gone dark."

"But you aren't sure?"

"I'm sure. He is also being cautious."

She sat forward slightly. "Are the two instances related?"

Rafe sat back in his chair. He attempted to look casual, but she saw the twitch in his lips when she'd asked the question. "Yes. The two situations are related."

Addy turned to Myles. They communicated silently as only long-time teammates, and cousins can do. Myles then asked. "Our mission here is to find out what Senator Jackson has on president-elect King. We were told Casper was made privy to this information but we weren't told that your boss, Wade Evans, was also made privy to it. How many others know about this information and where do we stand in all of this?"

Rafe's head swiveled to Myles. "It's my understanding that the only people who are aware of the dirt on the president-elect are, Senator Jackson, my boss Wade Evans, Casper, myself, and of course, you. Of course, it does seem, based on the senator's paranoia, there may be others who know he's been talking. His own behavior of late would also give that away, since he's been spitting and sputtering all over town about being stabbed in the back and more."

Rafe's phone buzzed and he glanced at the screen. "Senator Jackson is at home. The television is on and as of ten minutes ago, he let his dog out."

Addy nodded. "Is the senator married? Are there children at home?"

"He's married but I understand his wife left a few weeks ago and hasn't returned. They have two teenage children who are also with Mrs. Jackson."

Henry inhaled a deep breath. "We'll go and speak to the senator and find out what we can. Last night he was drunk and paranoid. In the meantime, please keep us apprised of any new information."

Rafe stood. "I must remind you that this is sensitive and confidential. You must not be found out. I have people watching the senator, but if anyone knows he's been telling tales, tall or not, they'll be watching him too."

Addy held her hand out to shake Rafe's. It was a way to dismiss him, and yet be professional and polite. But, she wanted to see if that same feeling came over her again when their hands met.

He wrapped her hand in his. His fingers squeezed around her hand, and her arm sizzled all the way up to her shoulder and down to her core. She saw him swallow. He felt it too.

"Thank you for coming, Rafe. We'll let you know what we find out from the senator."

"I appreciate regular updates. This topic is sensitive and if Senator Jackson really has dirt on president-elect King, King's team will shut it down any way they can."

"By any way they can, do you mean deathly consequences?"

Rafe swallowed, his Adam's apple rose then lowered. She watched his tie move with the motion. She wanted to kiss his neck, but his words brought back the reality of their situation.

"Let's just say, there are many suspicions swirling. In my line of business, where there's smoke, there's fire."

Myles shook Rafe's hand, then Henry. Addy stepped toward the front door, letting Rafe follow behind her. She swallowed a dry lump in her throat before turning to face him. "We'll be in touch."

"Be careful."

He stepped out the door and she watched his purposeful steps until he neared the street. She closed the door and squared her shoulders. She was lead on this mission, it was her time to shine.

"We need to find out what we can about president-elect King's 'team'." She used air quotes. "Who is associated with him in that regard? Was it that man in the bar last night with the red hair? We also need to start a file on Jackson's family. Where are they, are they in danger too? Is that why they aren't here?"

She moved toward the staircase. "If you two get Tate working on those things, we'll leave as soon as I've changed. I think we go to Jackson's place right away. Let's order some pizzas and I'll deliver them to the senator. You two will go around the back of his home and sneak in."

Myles grinned. "You're good Addy."

She shrugged. "We're all good, we've just been sedentary for a couple of years in Kentucky. Let's prove our worth once again."

Henry chuckled. "Sounds good. I'll work on the report upload for the family."

Myles headed to the dining area where their computers were arranged on the table. "I'll take the upload on King's team."

He sauntered in and Leesha greeted him.

"Good morning, Leesha. Anything on fire today?"

She laughed and shook her head. Her dark hair was twisted high on her head today. She wore small gold hoops in her ears and her red lipstick set off her dark complexion perfectly. She'd always been a classy dresser and that was the first thing he'd noticed about her when he hired her. It was a bonus that they could banter slightly and yet she never left without her work completed. In all, she was a find!

"Nothing on fire. Though you've had a few phone calls. All in the system. And your report on the Matthew matter is due in three days. I have the basic outline in the file."

He grinned and continued on to his office as Leesha added, "And your brother called."

"I'll call him back first."

He settled at his desk, booted his computer up, then

dialed his brother's phone. On the third ring he heard, "It's about time."

He chuckled. "It's nice to hear your voice too."

"Sorry. I'm standing in the store, looking at stuff and don't know what I'm looking for."

Rafe leaned back in his chair. "What kind of stuff?"

"Women's stuff. Lingerie. I mean, women look sexy in this stuff, but holy shit, there's numbers and letters and I don't know what any of it means."

Rafe tried stifling his laughter. "Why are you calling me? I don't know any more than you do."

"You've had a lot of girlfriends. I haven't. I need help here, Rafe. Tomorrow is Beth's birthday, our first one since we've been dating, and I need to get her something."

"Are you sure she wants lingerie?"

"Well." He heard Brett let out a long breath. "I don't know. I mean, do they like this stuff?"

"I don't know Beth that well, Bud. Usually, we buy that stuff for them because we want to see them in it. I've heard that women would prefer to buy their own lingerie, because they'll buy something comfortable to wear."

"Geez." Brett mumbled. "Then what am I supposed to do? I don't have time. I'm fucking up to my eyeballs in work and took my lunch hour to shop today."

"How about you buy her a gift certificate to a fancy store and put it in a box of her favorite candy."

"That's why I called you."

Rafe chuckled. "For the record, you could have called Brooke about the girly stuff."

"I'm not talking to our sister about women's underwear and sizes."

Rafe burst out laughing. "Fair enough. Besides being up to your eyeballs in work, how are you doing?"

"I'm good." He heard mumbling. "I got a call from Dad yesterday."

Rafe's spine stiffened. "What did he want? Money?"

"Yep. I told him to stick it up his ass. He's scheming some new business venture."

"That's what I would have done too."

"Hey bro, I've got to go. I'm checking out and can't juggle my phone and my wallet. I'll call you later today or tonight."

"I look forward to it."

He disconnected the call and stared at his computer. His mind instantly went to Adelaide Masters. He'd been correct before when he thought she was beautiful. In person, she was stunning. And smart. Maybe too smart. They were beginning to put things together. But, this was no ordinary situation and they needed GHOST's help.

His cellphone chimed. He pulled it up and glanced at the screen. It was one of his guys watching the senator. "What's going on?"

"I think there's trouble."

"What makes you think that?"

"I saw a man walk up the sidewalk and knock on the door. The door opened a crack and the man pushed the door open harder and let himself in."

"How long ago?"

"It happened about five minutes ago. I've been watching but I don't see anything going on."

"What kind of vehicle did the man come in?"

"No vehicle in sight. He walked up the sidewalk. There isn't a vehicle on the street in sight."

"Shit." Rafe rubbed his forehead with his fingers. "Go up to the house and listen for anything. Even knock on the door and ask for the senator. Keep me on the phone."

He listened to his man's footsteps. The boots he obviously wore made a thumping sound on the pavement. He could hear the knocking. His heart began racing as he listened. That man wasn't from GHOST, he'd bet that much. They were much better than that. If they went in, they wouldn't be seen. The doorbell sounded and his man yelled, "Hello. Senator?"

Silence was all that came back. His man then spoke through the phone. "No one is answering."

"Are you sure you didn't see the man come out?"

"I'm sure. I waited after I saw him push his way in."

"Stay put. I'm calling someone to check on things. Stay out of sight."

"Will do."

Rafe tapped Adelaide's number and listened to the rings. Before the second one, she answered. "Hi, Rafe."

"Hi, Addy. I have a man watching the senator's house. He said a man walked to the front door and knocked. The senator cracked the door open, and the man pushed his way in and hasn't come out. I had my man knock and ring the doorbell, but no one answered."

"When did this happen?"

"Five or ten minutes now."

"Is he still there?"

"Yes."

"Ask him to stay, we're on our way."

Rafe stood and paced his office. He couldn't focus on anything else. Then, he opened his laptop and entered into the secret server Wade had set up. He checked the geo tags for Wade and didn't see them lit up. So, he did go dark - good. Checking the last location he knew him to be, he was relieved he didn't light up. At least there was that.

He closed his laptop and turned in his chair to stare out the window. His phone rang and he swiftly answered.

"Martin."

"Mr. Martin, this is Matt Holden. I've run the sketch you gave me through our data base. A positive ID just came back. The man's name is Jensen Gable. He has a rap sheet, though mostly petty stuff. I'll email you what I found."

"Thanks, Matt."

He shook his mouse in impatience, waiting for the email to come through. The instant the email landed in his inbox, he clicked it open and watched as the photo populated. That was him alright. Reading through his rap sheet he saw a man with a colored past. Burglary. Property damage. Breaking and entering. Pickpocket. None of these things had anything to do with explosives. So he was either escalating or trying something new.

boiling and the [...] She hadn't had pizza in a [...] work at the HOG, made them healthy meals. Pizza hadn't made it onto her healthy delights yet. Hopefully one day though.

Pushing the doorbell a few times in frustration she leaned to the right and tried peering through the frosted glass on the side panel of the door. The frosting was good - it revealed nothing.

Something sounded from behind the door, then it cracked open. "Senator, I have..."

"Save it. It's me." Myles chuckled.

Myles stepped back but kept himself hidden by the door. Once she was inside, he twisted the lock on the door and shook his head.

"We've found blood. No body though."

"Show me."

Following Myles through the foyer and living room to

the kitchen, she saw small amounts of blood spatter on the refrigerator and cabinet alongside.

"He was shot." She guessed.

"Yes. But, he's too big to drag or carry. This was likely only a few minutes ago because the blood is still wet. And Rafe's guy saw someone come in."

Addy set the pizza box on the table, making sure there weren't any blood spatters or tracks and examined the area with Myles.

"Where's Henry?"

"Checking out the rest of the house."

"Okay."

She glanced around the kitchen, saw the back sliding doors ajar and pointed at them. "Is that you?"

"Yes."

"And you didn't see anyone out there when you came through the back?"

"No. We came from the neighbor's yard behind and didn't see anyone."

Addy glanced around the floor of the kitchen and saw the dog's water and food bowl. "Where's the dog?"

"Great question. So, someone came in here, shot the senator, he's gone and so is his dog. No signs of anything else."

She turned and searched the cabinets and doors in the kitchen. "I'll bet he has a safe room. A lot of these Washington mucky-mucks have them. They all have a ton of enemies."

Henry entered from the front hallway. "There's no sign of anyone upstairs. Four bedrooms. One clearly a guest room. One for a teenage boy and one for a teenage girl. Their school pictures and sports photos are in their rooms. The last is the master."

"Okay. Let's look down here. We're looking for entry to a safe room. It will be in the interior of the home."

Myles pulled his phone out and turned the flashlight on. He sauntered along the walls, shining the flashlight on the wall as he went. Henry did the same on the opposite side. Addy opened doors to the pantry, a butler's pantry, and the basement. "I found a basement. I'm heading down."

Henry stopped. "I'll go as backup. At my grandparents' house we have a safe room in the basement."

Henry stepped in front of Addy, flipped the light switch on, and moved deliberately down the stairs to the basement. Addy had her hand on her weapon, just in case and reminded herself to stop watching scary movies. In her line of work, there was too much weirdness in reality to watch stuff like that. Such as going into the basement.

At the bottom of the stairs, there was a sitting area, a television, two recliners, and a sofa. The walls held photographs of the Jackson family. On the far wall a full-length mirror reflected Henry and herself and a crack in the wall behind her.

She nudged Henry, who saw it at the same time. He turned and they approached the wall. He nudged her and nodded. Then he pointed to the corner where the wall met another wall at a ninety-degree angle. There was a collage of family pictures on the wall, but what looked like a wooden separator between the collage wall and the sofa was actually a facade hiding the control panel to open the door.

Henry slowly slid the panel open and grinned. "Any idea what the code might be?"

She shook her head. But Rafe supplied us with the

senator's contact information. I'll text him and see if he responds."

She tapped out a text to Senator Jackson.

"It's Adelaide from last night. I'm here to help you. Please let us in."

She sent the text and shrugged. Then she nudged Henry. "Text Tate. Maybe he can patch in with your phone remotely and run the code scanner on it."

Henry tapped out his text and she stared at her phone waiting for the Senator to respond. Myles came down the stairs and shook his head.

Addy pointed to the wall and Myles nodded. He then began walking around the basement looking into rooms and on shelves.

Her phone buzzed and she saw a text from the Senator.

"He's going to kill me."

"Are you in your safe room?"

The three dots bounced and finally one word appeared.

"Yes."

"We're outside your safe room. What's the code to get in?"

The dots started. Stopped. Started again. Then stopped. Finally a click sounded and the door opened.

The entire collage wall opened as a door, and the senator sat on a bed in the room, his shaking dog next to him. The dog growled as they entered, and the senator whispered to him. "It's okay, buddy."

There was blood on his shirt, between his shoulder and his collar bone. His left arm sat limply at his side.

Addy stepped forward. "I'm a medic. Do you have a medical kit here?"

The senator's faded blue eyes stared into hers for a moment then he nodded slowly. "It's over there." He nodded toward a bank of cabinets with his head, then winced. Addy pulled open drawers until she located a first aid kit. It would have to do.

"I need to remove your shirt to see if the bullet went through."

"He's going to kill me. King. He's going to do it. That man tried but Buddy here jumped at him. He ran out of the house through the garage."

Myles immediately hustled up the stairs.

"Okay. We're here now and we'll protect you." She looked for a pair of scissors and cut the t-shirt the senator wore above the bullet wound and down the back.

"No exit wound. I can't get the bullet out with a first aid kit. We'll have to get you to a doctor."

"A doctor will call him. He has the entire city at his beck and call. If I don't turn up dead, he'll have everyone out looking for me."

Addy glanced at Henry then worked on cleaning up the senator. It wasn't bad, as far as bullet wounds go. Sadly, she'd seen a lot of these in the military. She spoke to her teammates as she cleaned the senator up. "Small caliber. Little damage to the entrance."

Henry tapped his phone and exited the room. She could hear him talking to Tate as she bandaged the senator. When Henry ended his call, she asked, "Did your parents establish a doctor in town that would help in case of an emergency?"

"I'll call Dad."

11

"Are you the officer working my call?"

"One minute."

Some form of scratchy music blared through his phone and he pulled it away from his ear.

"Officer Mayes."

He straightened in his chair. "Officer Mayes, this is Rafe Martin. We spoke yesterday at the Alexandria gym after the explosion."

"Yes, Mr. Martin. I know I owe you a call, but we've been chasing down leads and working the investigation."

"I understand. That's why I'm calling. I had one of our sketch artists here at the DoD complete a rendering of a man I saw leaving the locker room yesterday just seconds before the explosion. I got a vibe from him when he left. The way he looked at me seemed as if I'd startled him. My locker had scratches on it as if someone had tried to get into it. I was chasing him down when the explosion happened."

"I'll need verification of the artist and authenticity."

"I've got that. I'll email it all over to you. I also ran this man through our facial recognition and Jensen Gable is his name. His rap sheet is long, but it's all mostly petty crime stuff. Burglary, property damage, B&E, and more. If he isn't on your suspect list, he should be."

There was silence on the other end of the line and for a split second, Rafe wondered if he'd hung up. "Okay Mr. Martin. Why don't you send over what you've found and I'll take a look."

He heard paper shuffling and a chair scrape the floor. "Mr. Martin, Jensen Gable is not on my suspect list.

"Will do. Give me your email address and I'll send it right now.

Rafe sent the email to the detective and checked his cell phone to see if he'd missed a call while talking to the detective. He knew he hadn't, but waiting was impossible sometimes.

He stood abruptly intending to pace his office once again when his phone rang.

"Adelaide. What have you found?"

"We have the senator, we're at his house. He's been shot. It's not life-threatening, but painful. From what I can tell the bullet entered near the clavicle. There's no exit, so I can't tell much, and don't have the proper medical equipment here to extract the bullet. We need a doctor. One that won't say anything to King or anyone else. The senator is convinced King has everyone in his pocket these days. Henry checked with his dad, they don't have a doctor here they can trust."

Rafe sat with a thud and closed his eyes. "I'll need to do a bit of checking. I'll call you in five minutes. Don't go anywhere until then."

"Roger." Then silence.

His pulse quickened as he logged into the secret server. If someone got to the senator in broad daylight, they weren't afraid of getting caught. According to his man, the assailant walked right up the street. He'd have to see if his man could describe him to the sketch artist.

Rafe's fingers deftly flew over the keys, the only thing slowing him was waiting for his computer to catch up and locate what he was looking for. They had people in place for everything. Over time they found it necessary. It wasn't only King and his ilk. Every powerful politician in this city was dirty in some way. They all had moles and people who needed a favor or owed a favor. Casper had decided to start their own network years ago, before his time here, to protect their assets and the job they did, so that no one else knew what they were doing.

He found the doctor's name and phone number, then called him.

"Hello?"

"Dr. Krueger, I'm calling for Casper. We need your services."

"What do you need?"

"Gunshot victim. No exit wound. Near his clavicle."

He heard the good doctor blow out a breath. "I can meet them in a half hour."

"I'll set up the room at the hotel. I'll text you the room number."

The line went silent. He scrolled his contacts and found the hotel's phone number. As he listened to the ringing, he checked the time. Casper hadn't checked in yet today.

"Lincoln Lodge."

"I need a room please."

"Sure. What date?"

"Today. As soon as possible. One night."

"Okay. I have one here for you. I need name, credit card, and license plate number."

"I'm calling for Casper. We have an account there."

"Yes. Thank you. Room 214. Same entry code."

"Thank you."

He hung up and texted Dr. Krueger the motel and room number. He dialed Adelaide's number.

"Hello, Rafe."

Inhaling a deep breath his brows furrowed. She elicited a response in his body every time he spoke to her. It was unnerving. "You're to take the senator to the Lincoln Lodge Motel. Room 214. Doctor Krueger will meet you there. He's one of ours."

"Okay. I assume he's done this before since you have everything pulled together so quickly."

"Yes. Sadly."

She huffed out a breath and he imagined her pretty face as she absorbed the information.

"Thank you, Rafe."

The line went silent and he felt deflated. Shaking his head he then called his man watching the senator's house.

"Yeah."

"They'll be taking him out of the house. Follow at a great distance. These folks are smart. I don't want them thinking I don't trust them, because I do. But I'd like you to watch their back a bit."

"Why do you want me to follow at all?"

"If they need assistance, I want you to let me know."

"If they're so good, why would they need assistance?"

Irritation raged through his body and he grew warm. "Just follow orders."

He ended the call, frustrated the days were over when he could slam the phone down on someone. The silent finger tap to his phone didn't hold the same appeal.

Sitting at his desk once again, he pulled up the brief he needed to work on. His head was not in this today at all. He read the same paragraph three times before deciding to call it and leave for a drive.

12

————

...stairs ...his groaning began to ...he was in pain, but honestly, this ...and bleeding wasn't going to help him. They needed to be out of sight in the motel room. Henry and Myles kept watch.

Finally reaching the door, she pushed the code into the electronic entry keypad and the door unlocked. Heading her over inside, she had him sit in an old vinyl chair at the table in the corner. Myles stood in the doorway. "You good in here?"

She grinned. "Yeah. I'm good."

He closed the door and she moved to the sink outside of the bathroom to wash her hands. She pulled a plastic cup from the plastic wrapper around it and filled it with water. She set that in front of the senator. "Drink this so you don't dehydrate. You've been through an ordeal."

The senator looked at her for a moment, then picked up the cup with a shaking hand. After drinking the entire glass of water, he set it down.

"Who are you really?"

"I'm someone protecting your ass."

"Who is protecting me? Are you planning on turning me over to King and his buddies?"

She sat on the corner of the bed and faced him. "No we're not turning you over to King. But I'm not at liberty to say more."

"Why are you protecting me?"

"We understand you have information on president-elect King, and that's what's gotten you shot and us here to protect you. What is that information?"

Faded blue eyes stared into hers for a long time. Before the senator answered the door opened and the spell was broken. If there was a spell.

A gray-haired man stepped into the room with a large medical case in his hand. "I'm Dr. Krueger."

"Hello, Doctor. Your patient here has suffered a gunshot wound to the clavicle area. No exit wound. The bleeding has stopped."

"Thank you."

He stepped over to the senator and laid his medical bag on the table. He glanced at the senator's shirt then glanced back at her.

She stood and began removing the safety pins she'd used to hold his shirt together after she cut it off. "I didn't have any choice and we didn't have time to get him a new shirt."

The doctor nodded. "Please turn on all the lights."

She moved around the room turning on every light she could find, though the room was still dim. Pulling her phone from her back pocket, she turned on her flashlight and shined it on the wound. The doctor gently pressed around the wound and the senator grumbled more than was necessary.

"Okay. Please pull the bedspread from the bed and lay the plastic sheet tucked in the side of my bag on the bed. Then help me get the patient on top of it."

The senator sat up straight. "You only use plastic when you're going to kill someone. I'm not..."

Dr. Krueger stood straight. "I've never killed anyone in my life. But, there will be bleeding when I remove this bullet and we don't need the hotel any the wiser. Since you're here and I was called, I believe this is a situation that needs to stay on the down-low."

"Yes, but I don't like..."

Addy finished opening the plastic sheet and covering the bed. She then laid her hand on the senator's good shoulder. "It's alright. I promise we aren't going to kill you. If we were going to do that, it would have been much easier to do it at your house."

The senator's cheeks, though previously pale, deepened in color. She urged him to stand by tucking her arm under his good arm and lifting. When he stood willingly, she let out a sigh of relief.

"Okay. Pull his shirt down to below his chest."

She managed to pull his shirt over his wounded shoulder, then down his left arm. Peeling the right shoulder off his body, she pulled his shirt down and tucked the remnants under his body.

Dr. Krueger stepped to the left side of the bed with a syringe and a small bottle of something.

"Don't put me out. You can't do that. Please..." The senator blustered.

The doctor looked him square in the eye. "Unless you want to feel every cut and tug and pull, I'm giving you a local anesthetic. You'll be awake, but you won't feel anything. Alright?"

"Yes." The senator's eyes landed on hers. "You'll be right here?"

"Yes. I'll be right here."

To his credit, the senator only flinched slightly when the needle poked his skin. She watched as the stressed look on his face began to relax and the pain subsided.

"See, that's better, isn't it?"

"Yes."

The doctor began pushing against the wound and the senator didn't so much as move. Then the doctor opened the wound with a scalpel, and she decided to keep the senator occupied.

"Can you tell me what information you have that has gotten you into so much trouble?"

"I can't. My only protection is keeping the information secure."

"If we can find it, we can keep it secure. It's our job to do so."

"I don't even know who you are. Who you work for. Or anything else about you. I'm not giving you that information."

Addy took a deep breath and looked away from the senator. She turned back to him, "I can tell you the person we work for is trying to help you. We also know we only have a couple more weeks until the inauguration and that information needs to be in the proper hands before then. Does that help you decide?"

"I told you, it's my only security. Plus I gave the information, verbally, to Wade Evans."

The door opened and she looked up to see Rafe Martin standing in the doorway.

The senator's eyes widened when he saw Rafe, but Rafe was only looking at her.

"Did you get the information you need?"

"No."

Rafe turned his deep brown eyes to the senator, then back to hers. Her tummy felt like butterflies had been let loose. Her heartbeat sped up and her breathing shallowed. He stood tall and handsome in his suit and tie. The breadth of his shoulders was impressive.

"I don't think we can protect him anymore. He clearly doesn't want to be protected."

"I was just thinking the same thing."

"No, no, I need protection. I need it. He's going to kill me."

Addy turned to the senator and lowered her voice. "We need your information to keep it and you safe."

A tear slid down the senator's temple as he stared into her eyes. "Just promise me this. If he gets me, please keep my family safe."

"We'll do our best. I promise you that. And, we're pretty damned good."

13

The senator filled them in on about the hidden lockbox. Addy questioned the senator as the doctor began stitching up the wound in his shoulder.

Addy nodded. "What's the security code to open the safe room and the lock box?"

The senator swallowed what appeared to be a lump the size of an apple. He let his breath out and said, "Both are the same."

Addy nodded but didn't write anything down and he was impressed. The doctor declared the extraction a success and she stood and pulled her phone from her back pocket.

"I'm going back to the senator's house to get the information. You guys need to stay here and guard him."

Rafe squared his shoulders. "You're not going alone."

"Why not?"

"What if King's men are at the house? You'll be there with no backup. No one to guard you."

The second she tilted her head and her lips formed a straight line across her face, he knew that was the wrong thing to say.

Henry coughed and tried to hide his amusement. The instant his eyes landed on Myles's though, he saw the humor. What in the hell did they think was so funny?

Addy slowly stood. Her shoulders pulled back and her spine was straight as an arrow. When her dark brown eyes stared straight into his, the little hairs at the back of his neck prickled.

When she spoke, her voice was even and low. "I don't need anyone to guard me."

Fear prickled his skin, something skittered down his back - fight or flight syndrome began to kick in. His palms began to sweat.

"I meant." He swallowed. He could barely hear his own words over the beating of his heart and the snickering of Henry and Myles. "I meant...It never hurts to have backup. You should have backup."

Myles nodded. "You should be her backup."

Straightening his spine, he nodded in return. "Okay." He braved a look at Adelaide. "Shall we go?"

She huffed out a breath but didn't say anything in return. Not to him, anyway. She turned to her teammates, "We'll come back here. The senator will need to rest after what he's been through. If you have any issues, let me know."

The senator finally found his voice. He watched Dr. Krueger close his case after carefully packing his blood-stained tools in a towel, then in a bag, and placed into his medical kit. Dr. Krueger met his gaze. "I'll sanitize them at the clinic. You'll feel a bit of pain when the numbing wears off. Take some painkillers, over the counter should suffice. Don't lift anything heavy for ten days or more. Change your bandage daily, keep your wound clean until it heals. If you need anything else, these folks can get in touch with me."

Dr. Krueger barely looked his way as he passed. Slipping out the door, he disappeared. His footsteps were quiet on the walkway outside. He was like a ghost in the night.

Senator Jackson sputtered. "Wait. What if they come for me?"

Myles turned to him. "Henry and I will be here."

"But this isn't safe. These walls are paper thin, that door could barely keep a mouse out."

Rafe agreed with him. This place wasn't secure. But for now, it was an unknown. Henry sat at the table. "We're working on a safe house for you. As soon as we have confirmation on that, we'll move you. Until then, we're here. You need to rest to get your strength up. So, take a nap."

Addy grabbed a large shoulder bag off a chair in the corner, then passed him as she stepped toward the door. She softly addressed Myles and Henry. "Call if you need anything. We'll be back soon."

Her eyes met his for the slightest moment before she slipped out the door as quietly as Dr. Krueger. Nodding he followed her out, deciding it was better not to say anything to her until he could gauge her mood.

At the bottom of the stairs she finally turned to him. "Where's your vehicle?"

"It's right behind you."

Her head turned, the smooth column of her neck caught his attention. Her profile was stunning. She began moving toward his vehicle and he followed without a word. Once again for the hundredth time in the past two days he thought about how his life was going to change. He had no idea how much and right now he was thrust into going on a recon mission for information. He hadn't been on a recon mission since his military days twelve years ago. Hopefully it was like riding a bike.

Once they'd both buckled up, he maneuvered his vehicle to the driveway of the motel. "I'll need an address or directions from you." He watched her lips turn up slightly.

She leaned forward and punched the senator's address into his navigation system. A few seconds later the robotic voice told him to turn right and get up on the expressway.

Merging into the traffic, he let out a deeply-held breath, and put his mind to the task and what he'd done in the past on missions. As his thoughts were organizing themselves, she interrupted them.

"You're right in that it's better to have backup. But, for the record, I could have slipped into the house unseen, gotten what I needed and slipped out without issue."

His eyes landed on hers for a moment. He dreaded looking away from her. She had a soft serene beauty that invited his attention. Not that she tried to get it. And that was the thing about her. She was guileless. She didn't seem to care if he noticed her or not. She was just who she was and that was likely the biggest appeal of all to him. He'd known plenty of women who played games and craved attention. Adelaide was just the opposite - attention would get her noticed. And a special operative didn't want to be noticed.

"I have no doubt you could perform your job at the

highest level, Addy. I just thought you should have someone watching your back."

Her head nodded slightly as she sat back in the seat. His back relaxed slightly as the heaviness of the previous few minutes subsided.

She smiled slightly. "Thank you."

14

nice that
costly, she didn't
hotel room with the senator.
They'd been stationary in Kentucky for the most part, now
she wanted to be out and doing things.

Glancing at him as he drove, her thoughts rambled
about. He was likely one of the handsomest men she'd
ever met. And she worked with some handsome men. But
they were... like them, but they weren't men. Well, they were
men, but she didn't think of them as handsome. Not in a
potential mate sort of way.

Rafe pulled off the highway and entered the presti-
gious neighborhood the senator lived in. There were a ton
of wealthy people in this state. She mused about the ratio
of wealthy to poor here. It was a city and state of such
stark contrast between the haves and have nots.

He turned onto the senator's street. "Keep going past
his house. Don't slow or look at it in any way."

"Okay."

She watched as they neared, without turning her head

or showing interest. No cars on the street. Some kids were playing basketball three doors down on a court in the side yard of a neighbor's home.

"Okay, drive around to the street behind his house."

Rafe nodded and she saw him swallow but he didn't question, and she liked that.

"After this next house, pull over and shut the car off."

Her eyes scanned the area as he followed her directions. Pulling a black cap from the bag she carried she reached back and scooped her long hair into a ponytail in the middle of the back of her head. She then twisted the ponytail and coiled it around and slipped the ball cap over her hair. She turned to see Rafe watching her closely.

"Take your suit jacket off and untuck your shirt. You need to look less business and more casual."

He reached to the left and pushed a button that moved his seat back. His arm reached around her seat as he leaned toward her but grabbed a gym bag from the back passenger floor. She caught the scent of his aftershave and closed her eyes. Sandalwood and citrus. He smelled fantastic. It was nostalgic in some ways, as her dad wore a scent similar to that when he dressed up to go out. Never on a mission. But, when her parents dressed up to go on dates, she remembered how he smelled and how much her mom loved that.

Rafe's arms moved around and she watched as he pulled his suit jacket off, then unbuttoned his shirt. She tried not to stare. But, it couldn't hurt to peek a little. Pulling his shirt off he then grabbed the bottom of his t-shirt and pulled it over his head. He quickly donned a t-shirt he'd pulled from his gym bag and then a stocking hat he had laying in the bottom of the bag. She saw his physique. It was far too short of a glimpse, but he was muscular and toned.

He leaned forward and slipped his dress shoes off and quickly tied on his tennis shoes.

"Not much I can do about the dress slacks unless you want..."

"No." Her throat dried right up. She swallowed. "No, that's alright. I think the other clothes look casual enough not to cause undue attention."

He grinned, and that she couldn't look away from. Dammit. He was a handsome man.

His eyes locked on hers and her heartbeat kicked up. "What now, boss?" He grinned, and that did nothing to get her mind back on the mission at hand.

She blinked. "See that line of trees and shrubs?" She pointed out her window with her thumb.

He ducked his head to look. "Yeah."

"We're going to walk along like a couple admiring the foliage. It's a community pathway to the park at the edge of this street. It also leads to the senator's backyard."

His grin broadened. "Nice. Okay. Let's go enjoy the plant life."

He sprung from his side of the vehicle and hustled to her door before she could open it. Opening her door, he grinned. "If we're a couple, I'd open your door and help you out."

He held his hand out to her, and she took a deep breath before laying her hand in his. The instant she did, the sizzle she'd felt before zoomed up her arm and did crazy things to her body. Everywhere.

She quickly stepped from the vehicle, tossed her bag over her shoulder and waited while he closed the door and hit the fob to lock it. He then turned and surprised her by taking her hand in his as they neared the tree line.

Her thoughts were a mess and she needed to have her head in the game, but she didn't want to let go of his hand.

As they sauntered along the trees, she softly explained their next steps.

"At the end of this tree line, we'll step through and skirt the edge of the senator's property. We'll stroll along to the back door. All of these yards are bordered by large cedars and other larger trees. Everyone wants their privacy while at the same time, running the country. I'll unlock the door and we'll slip in."

"If he gave you a key, why don't we go in the front door?"

"I don't know if they are watching the house."

"If they're watching, won't they also be watching the back door?"

"It's impossible to watch the back door because of how the yards are situated and the large trees block everything. So, they'll watch from both sides and the front."

"Okay."

"Those kids playing basketball up the street looked too old to be enjoying a driveway game."

"Good catch Addy. I wondered about them as well."

They entered the senator's backyard, then strolled easily to the back door. She pulled the key from her pants pocket and quickly unlocked the door. They hurried inside. She held her forefinger to her lips and padded softly across the kitchen to the garage door. The door handle had been drilled into and the lock and latch no longer worked. She easily pulled the door open and waited for anyone to notice.

Rafe stood to her left, against the wall just as she was.

No movement was noted, so she stepped into the garage and saw it was in the same condition it had been in when they brought the senator to the motel in his own car.

"Okay. The safe room is this way."

She moved toward the basement door and deftly slipped down the stairs. Rafe was impressive in his stealthiness. Entering the passcode on the safe room door, they dipped inside and she closed the door behind them.

"We're looking for the small lock box he has hidden under the cabinets. I'm thinking false bottom, but maybe not. This is his safe room, so he may have felt as though he didn't have to hide it that well in here."

Rafe began opening cabinets and running his hands around the perimeters of each one. She did the same on the opposite side of the bank of cabinets. The dust and cobwebs in these cabinets proved the family didn't use this room often. Maybe never once it had been set up.

"I have something." Rafe softly said.

Addy stood and neared him. He moved the small appliances on the bottom of the cabinet, then pushed his finger into a small hole at the back of it and pushed. The bottom of the cabinet lifted, and his smile broadened.

"That's brilliant."

"My house has one of these. When I found it I wondered why someone would need it. Just two months in this city and I knew how many people kept the darkest secrets of all their wrongdoings. I'd bet every house in this city has one of these hidden cabinets."

[illegible] It was all [illegible] how a cabinet [illegible] he wasn't proud of [illegible]

He lifted the box from inside the cabinet and placed it on the counter. Addy stepped forward, her scent was enticing. But, not as enticing as her movements. She was agile, sure of herself and yet she had a soft touch. That [illegible] was on the inside in spades. Her family taught her well. Being raised with operatives all around her embedded all that knowledge into her body. She was more than just a beautiful woman. And that was his kryptonite.

Addy lifted the lid on the box. "Hmm." She softly said as she set the lid on the counter near the box.

"What's that mean?"

"No dust on the box means it's been opened recently. Maybe placed here recently. I noticed the other cabinets were dusty and filled with cobwebs. That tells me the senator has been accessing this information recently."

"He told Wade he had proof of King's wrongdoing. I'm not sure if he brought him some proof for their conversation or not."

"Did Wade share anything with you?"

"Only that he may need to go off-the-grid for a while and he felt as though the senator wasn't bluffing."

Addy stopped looking at the files in the box and turned to face him. "Are Casper and Wade, one and the same?"

He stared into her pretty brown eyes for a few moments. "I can't answer that Addy."

"It would help us to know if we're protecting two people or three."

"Casper has GHOST to help him. Wade has other sources. Let's leave it at that."

His phone buzzed and he pulled it from his pocket. A text from a hidden number appeared on his screen.

"They sent me this about three minutes ago."

A picture populated of Wade's wife and daughter outside their home in Virginia.

His fingers rifled across the screen of his phone.

"Are they safe?"

The three dots bounced.

"I'm going to get them."

"Let GHOST get them."

He stared at his screen for a long time, his stomach tightened into a knot as he waited.

Then a response finally appeared.

"They are."

He inhaled a deep breath and pocketed his phone.

Addy watched him but before she could say anything her phone rang.

She tapped the screen then put it to her ear. "Masters."

He watched her eyes as she looked at the box before them. Then her eyes landed on his and held.

"Okay. I'm on my way back to the Bowman home."

She listened for a few seconds then responded. "Okay, send the address. I'm on my way."

She pocketed her phone, gently placed the lid on the box and tucked the entire box into her bag. "We have to go to a safe house. There was an attempt on the senator. Myles and Henry are taking him to a safe house out of town. Are you with me?"

He didn't need to think about it. "Yes." He'd be no good at the office, and now more than ever, he needed to help sift through this evidence and see just what the senator had on King, because things were getting real. "We need to get out of here. They'll come back to toss the place."

"That's what I was just going to say."

She tapped a black screen on the door in the safe room and a camera showed them the outer area of the room beyond. She tapped on the edges of the screen and pulled up differing cameras around the house. Her hand froze over the screen. "If we can figure out a way to get the images from this camera of earlier today, we can see the intruder. We can run him through a database and identify him."

"My security system at home is similar. May I?"

Addy stepped aside and he slid his forefinger along the bottom of the screen. A control ribbon appeared and he searched for the settings icon.

A couple of taps and he found the settings. Opening them up he noticed the URL for the upload, copied it, memorized it, then managed to change the upload to go to the private server he used. Pulling his cell phone from his pocket, he accessed the server and noted the upload in progress.

He then changed the pass code to the door.

Addy moved closer. "Why are you changing that?"

"If something happens and they get to the senator, they still won't be able to get in here."

"We have the evidence."

"They won't know that."

The grin that spread across her lips was enticing as hell. The thought of kissing her grew stronger as they stared at each other. He felt like he was trapped in a spell of some sort. But the spell was broken by the ring of a phone. Hers.

She answered, "Masters."

As she listened to her caller, he reluctantly finished what he'd been doing. The passcode was now seven numbers and two letters. He checked the cameras around the house to make sure they were still alone. He then logged out of the system and the camera went dark.

He turned to Addy, who stood back two steps, watching him. That spell began to fall over him again, but he shook it from his mind and nodded to her instead. "Ready?"

She pocketed her phone. "Yes. We're headed out toward Virginia. Are you sure you're with me? You can drop me at the Bowmans', and I can get out there myself."

"I'm with you."

16

—————

[illegible] near the [illegible] over her [illegible] the area and they slinked [illegible] the stairs that would lead them to the back door. She was a master at soft footsteps. She'd learned it as a little girl. When she was little, she'd watched her dad sneak up on her mom to surprise her. Addy had marveled at the soundless approach and asked him [illegible].

"Addy, in my line of work, being quiet is one of the most important aspects of getting in or out of someplace alive."

"Will you show me?"

He chuckled. "Sure."

They'd practiced every day he was home. She'd practiced sneaking up on her mom and her friends every chance she got. She felt like a ballerina with her soft approach.

At the top of the basement steps, she peered around

the door and listened. No sounds. Stepping across the kitchen floor to the back door. She twisted the doorknob slowly, pulled it open and stepped outside. Rafe was close behind her, his presence comforting and exciting at the same time. She tried remembering her last boyfriend. It was weird that she couldn't even remember his face anymore. It was back in Indiana, she'd just gotten out of the military, and had been hired by GHOST. Not that it was a surprise she was hired, it was a given all her life. But, she was feeling rather proud of herself anyway. She and Maya had gone out for a couple of celebratory drinks and a handsome man approached her and asked her to dance. She remembered he was handsome. But now all she but could see was Rafe's face.

As they moved across the lawn to the edge of the trees, he took her hand in his and hurried her along toward the vehicle.

She looked back and saw the group of men who'd been playing basketball were sauntering down the sidewalk, near the senator's home.

Rafe pushed at the shrubbery as they moved through to the back walkway along the park's edge. His long legs took one stride to her two, but his hand held hers firmly. Her left hand gripped the bag on her shoulder tightly, keenly aware that what she carried was going to blow this town wide-open. At least according to the senator.

The last five steps Rafe's pace quickened. He pulled his keys from his pocket and unlocked the doors before they arrived. Jerking open the passenger door he all but pushed her in and ran around to the driver's side. She turned to see the men running toward them along the row of trees. Rafe had the car started and pulling away from the curb before the men were close enough to do anything.

Addy turned in her seat and saw one of the men pulling a cell phone up to his ear.

"They're calling someone. They'll know your vehicle."

"Right."

"Go to the Bowman home. I'll get the rental we have there."

He nodded. "Enter the address in the navigation system please."

Addy deftly managed the navigation system as Rafe sped along the streets to the highway as fast as he dared. He turned down a side road, before their exit and she glanced at his face. His jaw was tight, his focus laser sharp. She turned in her seat again and saw a black SUV following them.

"How long has he been back there?"

"A couple of turns now."

She picked up her phone and tapped Tate's number.

"Vickers."

"We're being followed from the senator's home. Who can you call to divert our tail? We're on our way to the Bowman home to pick up the rental. Rafe's vehicle is now spotted."

"Okay, I've got you on screen. I'll call you when I have someone to assist."

The line went silent and she turned to Rafe. "Tate will have someone assist us. Just stay calm and keep doing what you're doing."

A grin spread across his handsome face and her heart began thumping in her chest. When he turned to look into her eyes, she felt it. Her body reacted like she'd been punched in the gut.

"You know, this isn't my first rodeo."

"Right."

She didn't know much about Rafe Martin, but she hoped to find out all she could.

Her phone rang and she tapped the speaker icon. "You're on speaker."

"I have an officer I trust on his way to you. Stay on course and head directly to the Bowman home now."

Sirens drew close and Addy turned her head to see the flashing lights behind the SUV following them. "I see him."

"Good. Call if you need anything else. I'm watching you on the computer."

"Roger."

She ended the call and glanced at the navigation system. They only had ten miles to go.

"How is he watching us on his computer?"

She grinned. "I'm wearing a tag."

Rafe nodded, but she saw his cheek round as a smile spread across his face.

"I didn't know you utilized tracking tags. That's smart."

She grinned, but said nothing.

As they approached the Bowman home, Addy directed him. "Go around to the street behind. The garage is back there."

She lifted her phone again and typed out a text to Catalina.

"Please open the garage door."

She watched her phone screen as the words appeared.

"Done."

"Okay, the garage door is open, as soon as we approach, drive right inside."

Rafe chuckled. "Nice."

He adeptly pulled his vehicle into the garage next to the rented SUV they had picked up when they arrived.

She jumped from the vehicle and wasted no time running to the driver's side. Tossing her bag into the back of the SUV, Rafe stepped passed her. "I'm driving."

"I'm capable of driving."

"I know you are. But, I insist."

"Maybe I insist." She plopped her hands on her hips as she felt her temperature rise.

Rafe stopped and turned toward her. He stepped close, very close. She felt the heat radiate off of his body, which was still encased in a tight t-shirt that showed his muscles off nicely. His dark eyes bored into hers and she swallowed. His body bent at the waist until his nose nearly touched hers.

"I insist more than you," he whispered.

Then, his lips touched hers. Lightly, softly. They fit far too good. Then he pulled back and stared at her. "I've been thinking about that since I first met you. But, seeing you in action - dammit, that's sexy and I didn't want to wait any longer."

"What about what I want?"

The slow grin that spread his full sexy lips made her breathing stutter.

His voice was low when he responded. "What do you want, Addy?"

No way was she going to tell him that. Not right now anyway. She was pretty sure she wanted it all.

"Not sure you can handle what I want, Rafe."

His smile grew larger and his eyes deepened in color, if that was possible. "Sounds fun."

He turned and hopped into the driver's seat as she stood stupefied at this encounter.

[illegible] poker [illegible]. But that little [illegible] made it even more so. She [illegible] something in him, and it was the first time in [illegible] very long that he felt alive. He lived each day, but now he felt it. He felt invigorated and eager for the next minute, then the next.

She finally climbed into the passenger seat. She [illegible] the address into the navigation system.

She turned her head to him, her dark shiny eyes bright with life. Her soft lips, so incredibly soft, formed a slight smile. "Keys under the mat."

He leaned down and pulled the keys from under the floor mat. Then realized he didn't need to insert the key into an ignition, it just needed to be near the vehicle to start. He braved a look at Addy, and her lips turned up into a saucy smile.

Shaking his head, he pushed the button to start the SUV, then slowly pulled it from the garage. Once he'd exited, she pointed to the visor where the garage door button hung, and he tapped it closed. The navigation system told him to get back on the highway, and he followed its directions, but kept an eye out for anyone who may have been watching from afar.

Addy settled back into her seat. "So, let me guess, Marines."

He ventured a glance in her direction, then grinned. "Yes." Navigating a corner, he then asked, "What made you think that?"

"You're very regimented. Your moves seem calculated and precise."

Shooting a gaze into the mirror behind he saw no suspicious vehicles following. "I'll take that as a compliment."

She nodded. He saw her eyes dart to the outside mirror to see behind them and knew she was vigilant as well.

"What about you? I'll say Army."

"Yes. I went into the Army because that's where Maya and Myles went."

"Did you try to stay together?"

Her chest lifted as she inhaled. "Yeah. But, I went into the medical corps and they were recon and recovery. So, we ended up being separated anyway."

"Yeah. It's hard to stay together. Even the buddy system, created to encourage enlistments, they brag about isn't foolproof."

She nodded. "That's so true." She twisted slightly in her seat. "Why the Marines?"

His right shoulder lifted and fell. "The few. The proud. The Marines." He chuckled. "I liked their commercial. It appealed to the part of me who wanted a different life far away from where I was."

"Why did you want a different life?"

He braved a glance at her before turning to the road once again. "Let's just say I didn't have the best family life."

"Oh." She was contemplative for a few moments. "Did you get it? The different life?"

He chuckled. "Let's just say I haven't had an afternoon this exciting in a long time. I'm doing well professionally. That wouldn't have happened had I stayed at home. I'm financially secure. That *certainly* wouldn't have happened if I'd stayed home."

"That's sad. But I give you credit for knowing that and getting out."

He thought about her words and let them sink in. She gave him credit. That was something to ponder.

"What about you? Why did you join the military? You have a great family."

She grinned and it was stunning. "I do have a great family. And a great extended family. But, if I wanted to work for GHOST, I needed to have military training."

"You didn't want to be a doctor?"

"No. I split the difference by going into the medical corps and becoming a medic. But working in a clinic or hospital every day all day long is too boring and sedentary for me."

A laugh burst from his belly. "I know a few doctors who work ER and Triage. They'd laugh in your face if they heard you say that. It's anything but boring and sedentary."

She chuckled. "I'll rephrase my words. I like being in the action. I like going off to different areas and saving people. I like that life."

Something hot built in the pit of his stomach at those words. She wouldn't be staying put at all. He'd finally met someone who intrigued him in the most interesting ways and she would be leaving when this mission was over.

He turned off the highway and onto a frontage road. The frontage road took them three miles down to a narrow lane then the navigation system announced, "You have arrived at your destination."

Addy tapped on her phone then instructed, "Keep going. At the clump of oak trees, you're to take a right on a narrow lane."

Slowly driving the SUV down the lane, he grimaced when the tree and shrub branches scraped the side of the vehicle. There'd be scratches for certain by the sound of the scraping. The lane was rutted and bumpy. It didn't look as though anyone had been down it in a long time.

"Okay, there's the oaks. Turn right."

He navigated the SUV to the right, the lane narrowed considerably and the scrapes on the side of the vehicle grew louder.

"This vehicle is going to be messed up for sure."

"We'll pay for it."

He let it go. It didn't need a response. But, he mused that she was used to this sort of thing happening and knew they'd make it right.

"Okay. There's a pile of firewood stacked to the left up ahead. We're to turn left after the woodpile and park on the west side of the cabin."

"Is it smart to have the senator out here in the boonies?"

"Where should we keep him, in the middle of the freeway?"

"Of course not. But out here there isn't assistance if you need it."

She pointed out of the windshield. "There's my assistance."

Myles and Henry stood on the porch of the little cabin. They made it look far too small. Henry was big like his dad and he commanded attention when he stood like he was now. Arms crossed, which made them look massive. And that scowl he wore would scare away most people. He was a sharp contrast to the visage he bore. He was actually a great guy.

He stopped the vehicle and put it in park.

"Rafe, turn it around and back it into the spot. Easier for a getaway if we need it."

He did as he was instructed, a bit irritated with himself for not thinking of it himself. It had been so long since he'd done anything like this. His military career led him into the law and the law of politics, not personal protection and surveillance. He hired people for that now.

As soon as he shut off the SUV, Addy jumped out without waiting for him to open the door for her and strode to Myles and Henry. He watched her confident stride, her straight back and small frame, and he was impressed all over again.

appeared."

around them as he pulled into the lot at the motel. It stopped beside the senator's car and waited. I stepped inside and warned Henry trouble may be coming. We watched from the window as the man walked around looking in windows of the motel. Then he began trying to open doors. We got the senator up and ready to run. I walked down and approached him, asked him what he was looking for. Words were said. A bit of shoving ensued. Then he got a fist in his face and took off. I had Tate run his plate and it was the vehicle that apparently followed you earlier."

"How did he know to come here to the motel?"

"Great question."

Myles still stared at Rafe. Henry uncrossed his arms and took a deep breath.

"Where's the senator?"

Henry's thumb pointed over his shoulder. "He's sleeping. He's sore. And, between us, he's a baby. He huffs and puffs and moans more than anyone I know. You'd think he'd be grateful we're saving his ass."

Addy grinned. "I'm going to take a wild guess on this one and say this is way out of his realm."

Henry chuckled.

Myles addressed Rafe. "Are you here to help us or to keep track of us."

The hair stood on Addy's arms at Myles' tone.

She opened her mouth to say something, but Rafe spoke first.

"I'm here to help you."

"In what way?"

Rafe stood to his full height and faced Myles head on. "I'll remind you I'm military trained. I may be an attorney now, but I've been with the DoD for years. I train regularly, I shoot, and for the record, of the four of us, I'm the only one who knows all the players and what's happening here."

Myles' lips twitched at the corner. "That so? Then what is it the senator has on King?"

Rafe pointed to the bag slung over her shoulder. "Why don't we go in and find out."

It was time to end this posturing. She ascended the two steps to the porch where Myles and Henry stood, gave Myles the evil eye as she passed, then stepped into the cabin. Three pairs of feet followed her into the small space.

Her eyes adjusted to the dim light. Perusing the inside she noted four doors that led from this main living room. Henry moved toward her and pointed to the doors.

"That one is a bedroom and where the senator is sleeping. The one to the left of it is another bedroom. It has two queen beds inside. So does the senator's. The third door on that wall is a smaller bedroom with one bed inside. The last door over to the far right, is a bathroom. The kitchen is to the right and has most of what we'll need for a few days."

"Okay." She took it all in, noted their laptops on the table to the right of the living area, just in front of the kitchen and nodded. "Let's pull this stuff from the box Rafe and I recovered from the senator's house and see what we have. We need to assess a few things. First of all, how damning is this information? Second, if it's as bad as the senator thinks, where are we going to take him to secure him. We can't stay here long. Third, how is he being tracked? Did you search his car for tracking?"

Myles moved toward the table and sat in one of the chairs. "I scanned it. Nothing found."

Addy nodded. "Okay. So, we have to figure out how they are tracking him."

Her phone rang and she answered quickly. "Masters."

"It is Catalina. There are men trying to get into the house."

"Have you called the police and are you safe?"

"Yes. I called. I'm in the safe room. But I'm scared."

"I'll see if I can find someone to get there faster. Stay in the safe room."

"Okay."

Addy stepped toward Myles. "Call Tate and get Capital Police to the Bowman home. Catalina is in the safe room scared. Someone's trying to break in."

Myles pulled his phone up and called Tate. Turning to Henry, she said, "We need to find out who's there. The senator was never at the Bowman home, so how would anyone know to go there?"

"I'm on it." He started toward his computer and

stopped. "Maybe I should go back to the house. I'll run trackers on everything. First, I'll run a tracker on our rental to make sure it's not being tracked. It was in the garage at the house."

"Sounds good." She looked at Rafe. "Who in your office knows where you are?"

His brows furrowed. "No one. Are you suggesting I'm getting the senator tracked?"

"I'm not suggesting anything Rafe. But, we have to explore all avenues. Who in your office would know where you are?"

"No. One." His tone was clipped and she could see the anger filling his eyes.

"Your phone can't be tracked? Your computer?"

He jerked his phone from his back pocket. "Scan it."

Henry took Rafe's phone gently from his hand and plugged it into his computer. He watched the screen for a few seconds and shook his head. "Clean."

Addy picked Rafe's phone off the table and unplugged it from Henry's computer, then handed it to him. "I'm sorry. We have to be sure."

He took his phone from her, careful their fingers didn't touch, which made her sad, and pocketed his phone.

Henry stepped toward the door. "I'm on my way back to the house. Let me know if anything happens. I'll be back as soon as I can."

Myles ended his call with Tate. "Tate has police on the way."

Henry waved, then disappeared out the door. Addy took a deep breath and let it out slowly. She moved to the sofa and the coffee table in front of it. She moved the few magazines, which were a couple of years old, to the floor as well as the figurine of a bluebird. Pulling the box from her bag, she set it on the sofa and opened the lid.

Rafe sat on the other side of the box on the sofa. She looked into his eyes, her pulse quickened. She was getting used to that feeling when she looked at him. She liked how it felt for another human to make her feel alive.

"I'm sorry Rafe. I'm doing my job."

He bit the inside of his bottom lip before responding. "I understand."

She smiled softly. "Okay. Let's pull this out and see what we have. We may have to organize it in some fashion, but first, let's see what is here."

"Just tell me what you want me to do." His voice was deep and rugged and goosebumps formed on her arms and her chest. She felt the skitter of excitement slide down her spine. She knew what she wanted him to do to her. For sure. Since he'd kissed her she'd wondered about him. How he'd feel against her body. Since she'd seen him without his shirt, she knew his hard chest pushed into her would feel exciting. The heat that rolled off his body when she was close called to her. The last time she'd had carnal thoughts like this had been years ago. It felt like a lifetime though.

19

If he were

do the same thing

he sat next to her, working

beside her filling.

He scanned the documents in his hands. Text jumped out at him and a sizzle of dread skittered down his spine.

"My God." He turned toward her, a set of documents in his hand.

"What have you found?"

He looked into her eyes and spoke softly. "According to these documents, then Senator King, now president-elect King, traded oil contracts that he made millions on, for power in Yerezdan and gave the Prime Minister of Yerezdan sensitive information and access to our military contacts here."

Addy stared into his eyes as she held her hand out for the papers. Finally looking away, he watched her as she read them. She swallowed a few times and he was enamored with her profile. Her throat constricted and loosened when she swallowed and he imagined she was feeling the words she was reading.

Reading the last document, she slowly turned her head toward him. "This is bad."

"Yes."

He handed her another stack of documents he'd found earlier, which now made more sense. "This is worse."

Her movements were slow as she pulled the stack of documents from his hand. It was almost as if she were in slow motion. When she spoke, her voice was softer than a whisper. "Oh my God. King had the Chief of Staff of Yerezdan murdered."

"Yes." He motioned toward other documents. "The senator is complicit in keeping it quiet. He was used to funnel documents back and forth to Yerezdan. He was appointed the special envoy of Yerezdan and carried documents, and money, back and forth between the countries. That's why King is after him."

"But the senator is guilty of conspiracy. He's implicating himself."

"Yes. He doesn't care. Senator King promised to stump for Jackson. He didn't. Jackson believes there was a conspiracy to make sure he didn't win his campaign, to push him aside. When he threatened to tell what he knew, he became a target. His primary goal here is to make sure the president-elect isn't sworn in."

"These documents are his only currency right now."

"Yes. We need to scan them and save them on computers in case they are found."

He watched her bright eyes process what he'd said. Myles was listening to them and turned in his chair to face them. Addy glanced at Myles. "We'd have to have these certified as real."

"The best thing we can do is record the senator certifying each document."

"We need to do it right away. If he's being tracked somehow, we don't have a lot of time."

"Do you have protected servers?" Rafe watched Addy turn toward him, her brows furrowed slightly then unfurrowed. "We do."

"How about double security?"

"What do you mean by that?"

"Wade has a section of our DoD server masked and encrypted. Only he and I have access to it. It would be safe there as someone would not only have to get through the DoD firewalls, they'd then have to hack through the firewalls Wade put up around our secure server."

Carefully setting the documents on the table in front of her she turned her body toward him. Her hands folded in her lap as she stared into his eyes. "Why would you need a secure section of a server working with the DoD?"

He leaned back slightly and opened his body toward her. He'd felt disconnected from her a while ago, he wanted that connection back. "Not everyone who works at the DoD is trustworthy and Wade is fully aware of that."

She nodded then turned to Myles. "What are your thoughts on this?"

Myles stood and stretched his back. "I think it can't hurt. They'll move to destroy these documents the instant they get them."

"I'd like to speak with Casper about this. Can you have Tate ask him to call us?"

"Sure thing."

Rafe leaned forward. He put his hand on Addy's knee.

He wanted the connection with her. "We don't have much time."

"I know."

She tried smiling, though it was forced. She stood and padded to the senator's room. Slowly opening the door she disappeared for a few moments and he was bothered by that. Jumping up from the sofa, he sauntered to the senator's room and opened the door. Addy stood next to the bed as he grumbled about being awakened.

"Get up, Senator." He barked. Four startled eyes turned back toward him. "We don't have time for you to lounge around."

Addy turned to the senator. "He's right. Somehow you're being tracked."

The senator blustered. "What. You're supposed to protect me. How can you let this happen?"

Rafe had enough of the senator's disrespect and lack of gratitude.

"Get up or I'll jerk you up. These people are protecting you. Now you need to ensure the documents we've found will do what you intend for them to do."

The senator struggled to a sitting position, then twisted to stand. Addy stepped closer to him and offered support. For some reason, this irritated Rafe more than anything else. But he also felt pride. She was a caretaker no matter the circumstances. He admired that.

Rafe turned and exited the bedroom when Myles' phone rang. "Sager."

Myles' eyes flicked to his, then behind him to Addy. "Okay."

Addy settled the senator in the armchair at a right angle to the sofa.

Her voice was even. "What is it?"

Myles' eyes flicked to Addy's. His lips formed a straight line across his face then turned down into a frown. He turned his head and stared straight at him.

"Rafe's gym bag had a tracker on it."

His heart hammered in his chest and his stomach rolled. It was he who brought danger on them.

"What kind of tracker?" His voice wasn't as strong as he'd hoped.

"It was a tile. Easily purchased by anyone. Not professional at all."

"Does Henry have it?"

"Yes."

"Ask him to meet me at the DoD. I'll run diagnostics on it and find out where it originated and possibly who slipped it in my bag."

"You can't possibly think they're stupid enough to put their information on it?"

Rafe sucked in a chest full of air and squared his shoulders. "No. But, if they by chance paid with credit or debit cards, that information may be on there. The store it was purchased from is traceable from it. The date of purchase, the time even. We may be able to track him or her down through store camera footage."

Addy stepped to him. "Why is someone tracking you?"

20

He refused to go when she asked. "What are you hiding?"

He let out a deep breath and swallowed. "The day before yesterday I went to the gym for an afternoon swim. It wasn't planned, and not the gym at the DoD. When I left the pool and the changing room, I saw a man leave. He looked at me and his expression was surprised, which struck me as weird. When I got to my locker, I noticed it had been carved up as if someone was trying to get inside. I ran out to follow the man and just as I reached the lobby, he was exiting the building. Then an explosion happened in the area around the pool. It created mass chaos and confusion. I ended up helping people out of the building. When I was able to retrieve my belongings from my locker, it was a few hours later and I was exhausted and wired. I didn't think to check my bag for trackers as I didn't think my locker had been opened."

Myles stepped toward Rafe, his back stiff and his mood dark. "Why the fuck didn't you tell us any of this before?"

"I didn't think one thing had to do with another."

"Why would someone target you?" Myles' voice rose, his face tinted red.

"I don't know."

Addy took a breath and stepped between Myles and Rafe. She turned to face Rafe. "Do they think what the senator told Wade, he also told you?"

"It's possible."

The senator finally spoke. "I didn't tell Rafe anything."

"But they might think Wade told Rafe." She mused.

Rafe's voice softened. "Not if they know Wade. He's the most secretive man I've ever met. If you told him a secret, he'd take it to his grave."

The senator leaned forward in his chair. "I hope not. I told him about King so he'd do something about it before that son-of-a-bitch is sworn into office. Wade is also the most patriotic man I've ever known. He has integrity. Swearing in a corrupt president isn't something he'll allow."

The senator's face was pale. The skin under his eyes drooped. And, he was likely in pain.

She turned to Myles. "We need to begin having the senator certify these documents."

Myles nodded, then turned to his laptop, still open on the table. He tapped a few times, then pulled a camera and cords from a duffle bag near his chair. He set them up on the table, then pulled the table closer to the senator.

As he readied the senator, she looked into Rafe's eyes. "We need to talk."

Rafe nodded and she pointed toward the door. He

held his hand out for her to proceed him. As she stepped toward the door, her stomach tightened.

Out on the covered porch, she leaned against the rail, her arms folded together as they laid on the top. She inhaled the fresh air out here. The cabin was nestled deep in the woods, which was great for hiding, but it was also secluded. That wasn't good.

Rafe's footsteps neared her. He placed his hands on the rail before him, next to her. She hesitated a moment, irritated with herself for her mixed feelings.

"Rafe, you need to tell us everything that's going on."

"I can't Addy. Wade has trusted me with things that are not to be shared."

"We need to know what's going on or we're working in the dark."

She turned to face him, her arms crossed in front of her.

He turned and shoved his hands in his pockets. She swallowed the lump in her throat. She was exhibiting closed off body language, he wasn't.

Uncrossing her arms, she instead tucked her thumbs into her back pockets and looked Rafe in the eyes. Admitting to herself again how nice his eyes were, she allowed herself to stare for a few moments. He was an incredibly handsome man. Her heartbeat increased and it felt like she had bubbles in her tummy.

"Rafe. We need to come to some understanding. I get that Wade shared confidential information with you. But we can't put the senator, ourselves, or you in danger by only having some of the information."

She saw his chest rise and fall and her mind snapped back to when he changed his shirt and she'd seen his muscular chest.

"Addy, I don't want anyone to be in danger either. My ability to keep confidential information just that, is a source of pride for me. It's also why Wade shares things with me. He knows I'll be discreet."

"I can't believe even he would want anyone to get in the middle of all of this and get hurt or worse."

"No, he wouldn't. But, until I speak with him, I can't say anything further."

She swallowed to moisten her throat. He was incredible.

"What about the man who you believe bombed the gym, or at a minimum, messed with your locker?"

"I had a sketch artist draw him. Then we ran it through the computers at the DoD. He's been identified as Jensen Gable. He's a petty criminal with a long rap sheet. I gave his likeness and name to the police department."

"Any word on whether they've found him?"

He shook his handsome head, the dark hair now falling on his forehead. The sides were buzzed short, the look suited him. "I haven't heard from them."

"Do you know why he targeted you?"

Rafe inhaled a deep breath. "I don't think he meant to blow me up at all. He had the opportunity to do that when I was in the pool. I think he meant to create a distraction, which worked. I'd even lost my common sense for a while in not securing my things. By the time we'd gotten scared gym patrons outside and interviewed with police, I was eager to get out of there."

"When you left the gym, where did you go?"

"To the office. Then home."

"Did you take your bag home with you?"

"Yes."

"So, he likely knows where you live now." She watched

his face. His jaw twitched and clamped tighter, but he said nothing.

"Doesn't that bother you?"

"I have security. I live in a gated community, so I'm not too worried."

"He set off a bomb."

"A small one for a distraction."

She watched him for a while longer, then took a deep breath. "Call Wade. Find out what you need to find out. We need to share information, and I have a feeling it won't be safe here for long."

...and took [illegible] there was [illegible] places for people to [illegible].

He pulled his phone out of his pocket and tapped Wade's number. It rang twice and he worried he'd have to wait a few hours to talk to him. But as the third ring sounded, Wade's voice answered.

"Hi, Dane. What's happening?"

"I'm at a cabin in the woods outside of the city with the GHOST team and the senator. There was someone snooping around the hotel and they felt it prudent to move the senator to a safe house."

Wade's deep exhale of breath was the only sound for a moment. "Okay. What do you need from me?"

"Addy wants me to share what I know. We found the senator's paperwork, we have it here. I know what he's done and what he has on King. They are recording the senator now certifying and explaining the documents and how he knows them to be true in case he expires."

"Is he alright?"

"He was shot in the shoulder. He's in pain. But he's overweight and all this stress can't be good for him. Addy also believes we'll be compromised here soon and the senator will need to be moved again."

"Okay. It'll come out soon enough I guess. I have Gaige and company, from GHOST, out picking up my wife and kids. I was sent a photo of them outside of the house. King's men are watching them, it's better if they are secured."

"What about you?"

"I'll be joining them while I figure out how to expose King. I think Addy's right, you'll likely need to get the senator out of the state and somewhere secure. I'll talk to Gaige about it."

Rafe swallowed the lump in his throat. It felt like a giant ball of dirt going down, but he needed to tell Wade what happened.

"They tracked us to the Bowman home. It was because of me. There was a tracker in my gym bag."

"Jensen Gable was after you."

"It appears so. I didn't think he was previously. But..."

Wade huffed out a breath. "They're running scared right now Rafe. I don't believe anyone is safe. Do you have anyone in your office who you suspect would be on the take?"

"The only two people in my office are me and Leesha. Outside of us, the only others we deal with on a regular basis are the two interns, Ridley McCleskey and Brett Selisen. They've been in the office with us for two years."

"Remember what I told you when you first started with me, Rafe. There are so few people you can truly trust.

Most others are in it for the fame or the money. You need to find out what those two interns have going on in their lives. Do they need money? Is something else going on? Look at podcasts or someone trying to make a name for themselves."

"Okay. I'll take care of it as soon as we hang up."

"Rafe?" Wade exhaled. "You need to check out Leesha also. Something could have changed in her life too."

Rafe's stomach twisted. Leesha had always been stellar. She was also loyal.

"Rafe?"

"Yes. I'll check her out too."

"Okay. I'm going to be working on how to get the senator's information into the hands of someone who can get it to the correct people. As soon as you have the video uploaded of the senator describing what he did and each of the documents, send it to me on the private server."

"I will. It shouldn't be too much longer."

"Also from this point on, let's keep communication going through GHOST. I don't want King finding either of us. Does Leesha know where you are?"

"No. I only told her I was out."

"Cut off communication with her until you've researched Leesha and the interns. I'll have GHOST make contact privately and have her clear your calendar."

"Okay. Stay safe Wade."

"You too, Rafe."

The call ended and his gut twisted again. Time to get himself back into military mode.

He turned toward the door to the cabin when a movement in the trees caught his attention. He froze to see if it continued and signaled a rabbit or a squirrel in the trees.

Silence. Dead silence. Then he noticed even the birds had stopped chirping and he jumped for the door. Scampering inside he saw Myles and Addy turn toward him alarmed at his action.

"I think we have company."

Myles jumped up from his chair in front of the senator and picked up a bag laying on the floor against the wall. Addy moved toward the bag as well. Myles pulled out weapons and ammo. He handed Addy a long gun and a loaded ammo magazine. He pulled another long gun and a loaded magazine from the bag and glanced at him. "Your shooting skills up to date?"

"Yes."

He twisted the gun in his hand and Rafe moved across the floor in three long strides. He took the proffered gun and magazine in his hands and moved to the door. He inserted the magazine into the gun, cocked it to load a bullet into the chamber and peered out the window next to the door.

Behind him Addy and Myles did the same with their weapons and the senator whimpered lightly. Addy spoke to the senator softly. "I know you don't feel good, but you need to muster all your shit and get ready to run if we say run."

He didn't hear the senator respond, but he could see in his mind the face the senator was likely making. For someone who took it upon himself to schlep incriminating documents to and from Yerezdan, he sure wasn't the bravest of souls. Which made Rafe think about his conversation with Wade. He turned to face the senator.

"Why did you do it?"

The senator's eyes were red-rimmed and faded. His

face was ruddy but underneath that ruddiness was a paleness to his face that was rather sad. "Money and power."

"Was it worth it?"

The senator halted and stared at him for a few moments. All he did was slowly shake his head.

...senator.

...frightened. People

...and money.

He looked ... to hers for a moment, then he took a deep breath.

"What's your call?"

"One of us stays inside to protect the senator. The other two need to go out the back door and see if we can ... What did you see?"

"Nothing. I heard something in the woods to the west. Then, the birds stopped chirping and everything grew quiet."

Addy swallowed. "Okay. Rafe you stay here with the senator. Myles and I will see if we can push our guest to show himself." She stepped to the duffle bag on the floor and pulled out three comm units. Handing one to Myles, she hurried to Rafe and handed him the second one. Leaning her gun against the wall, she opened her comm unit to show Rafe what to do.

"Insert the earpiece. Turn this pack on and clip it to

your belt. The button on the outside of the earpiece is where you can turn it off and on."

"Okay." He inserted his comm unit and nodded to her. She tested. "One, two, three."

He nodded. She turned to Myles and he gave her a thumbs-up.

Rafe stared at her for a long time. "Be careful."

Her lips twitched. This was her bailiwick. This and her medic skills. "I will. You too. Be aware. Stay vigilant. If someone tries coming through the door, get him out the opposite door and to the vehicle. No matter what happens, get him out. Then, call me and I'll figure out where you should go."

"What about you? And Myles?"

"We'll be fine. This is what we do. We have the senator's car, we'll get out as soon as we can."

She turned to the senator. "Stand up and get ready just in case. Every second will matter."

The senator pushed himself to the edge of his seat. He'd stopped whining and mumbling. She took that as a good sign.

Addy turned to Myles, who'd just packed up the laptop and camera as she gave orders. "Ready?"

"Yep."

He'd pulled a dark hoodie over his t-shirt. She nabbed her dark hoodie off the back of the chair at the table and slipped it over her head. She reached into the duffle bag and pulled out a second magazine, tossed it to Myles, then pulled up another one for herself and tucked it in her back pocket.

Gripping her gun once more she looked to Rafe. She strode to the back door and peered outside through the glass top, saw no movement, then slowly opened it up, grateful it didn't squeak.

Pushing her back to the wall, she moved down the two steps to the ground, then propelled herself to the relative safety of the cover of the woods. Myles was right behind her. Once they'd stepped into the woods a few feet, she pointed to her right then to Myles. She pointed to herself then to her left. They'd split up now and see what they could flush out.

She listened with each slow step she took. Rafe was right, it was eerily quiet. She picked her footfalls carefully. A light breeze picked up and she was grateful and annoyed at the same time. The movement of the trees camouflaged her movements, but the wind also made it difficult to hear anyone else make noise.

Myles' voice whispered over the comm unit. "100 feet."

She moved herself to the small pile of firewood directly to the west of the cabin. "Woodpile." She whispered.

A stick snapped and she froze. She whispered, "Footsteps."

Ducking down she listened to the direction of the now discernible footsteps to her left. She ducked her head around the woodpile to look in that direction and she saw the movement through the trees. A man wearing navy blue pants and a matching jacket moved behind the large oak tree near the driveway.

She whispered to Myles. "One. Navy clothing. Large oak."

Myles responded. "Got him."

Then she saw a second man ducking behind a pile of rocks at the edge of the front yard. "Two." She whispered.

Myles responded. "Ten-four."

Peering around the woodpile, she lifted her gun to lay on a protruding log to steady herself. Tilting her head to peer through the scope, she sited in the man behind the rocks. Whispering, "Behind the rocks. Got him." She waited for him to show enough of himself to be a target. Her heartbeat increased slightly, but she exhaled slowly and forced her body to calm as she'd done many times before.

Her vision through the scope captured the man creeping toward the corner of the porch on the east side of the cabin. He used the vehicles in the driveway as cover. The instant he moved from the senator's car toward the SUV they'd rented she slowly pulled the trigger toward her.

BANG.

The sound rang through the air and a split second later the man behind the oak began to run toward the cabin. Another BANG rang through the air and she saw the man fall to the ground.

The man she'd shot, tried standing but she wanted to keep him alive.

"Myles. Man one is trying to stand. I'm going to zip-tie him and question him."

"Ten-four." She heard Myles' footsteps as he ran toward his man. She stood and slowly neared the wounded man wobbling on his feet. The instant his eyes met hers he dove toward his weapon and she raised hers. "Don't do it."

He continued to scramble. He now crawled on the ground, toward his weapon and she fired a warning shot over his head. He froze for a split second, then tried again.

Plunging ahead toward the man, she grabbed him by the ankle and dragged him back a few feet from his weapon. Pulling a zip tie from her back pocket, she tied his ankles together, then squatted over his back and dragged his left arm behind him. His right arm flailed around, forcing her to work for it. He twisted his body and partially turned under her, his right hand connecting with her jaw.

Myles ran to them, grabbed his right arm and twisted it back to lay on his left wrist and she zip-tied his hands tightly together.

Rolling him to his back, she assessed the wound she'd graced him with. The small hole in his upper right chest had a small amount of blood that had seeped onto his jacket. She unzipped his jacket and pulled up his t-shirt to assess the wound.

The skin had cauterized from the heat of the bullet and likely because of his poor man's armor, which was his jacket and t-shirt, it didn't go in deep enough to do major damage. It'd hurt for a while and he needed to have the bullet removed, but he wouldn't die.

"I want him tied to the porch railing."

"Gladly." Myles grunted as he dragged the tied man toward the cabin.

She rubbed her jaw where the jackass had hit her. Maybe she'd have a bruise tomorrow.

[illegible] out the [illegible] him he didn't [illegible] couldn't see Addy or Myles.

His heart was in his throat. Focusing on his breathing he strained to see Addy. Where was she? He twisted the deadbolt on the door. They could still shoot their way in, but it would slow them up enough that he could get the senator out of here. Hopefully.

"[illegible]"

The senator's eyes were wide, his voice garbled.

"A man down. Not one of ours."

"Geez-is." He mumbled.

Rafe peered out the window again and saw her. Addy was nearing the man on the ground, he was scrambling for his weapon. She was steady in her steps, her gun trained on him. She fired a shot above his head and it caused him to drop for a moment and then he began scrambling toward his weapon again. Rafe's fingers hovered over the deadbolt. He could shoot that man if he tried shooting Addy. He watched her steady progress toward the man, then she grabbed his legs and pulled him away from his weapon. In short order, she'd zip-tied his feet together then jumped on his back and pulled his left arm behind him. They wrestled with his right arm. Her head jerked back but Myles jumped in and jerked his arm back to his left arm. Addy secured his wrists together.

She stood and rubbed her jaw but followed Myles as he dragged the man to the porch.

Rafe twisted the dead bolt and pulled the door open. "What about the other one?"

Myles glanced up at him. "Dead."

Rafe moved to the back door and twisted the dead bolt on the door to secure it. Then scampered through the cabin to the front door. He stopped before walking out and turned to the senator. "You can sit down and try to relax."

"Thank God." He mumbled as he sat gingerly in the chair.

Rafe stalked toward Addy and Myles, eager to help them out. His blood thrummed through his veins, his heartbeat was still wild.

Addy looked the man in the eye. "Who sent you here?"

"Fuck you."

"Who's paying you?"

He pressed his lips together.

"How did you find us?"

The man began laughing. A little more than he should have. It was almost maniacal.

Myles reached forward and pressed his knuckles against the man's wound.

He yelled out, but Myles didn't stop pressing.

Addy asked once again. "How did you find us?"

The man's voice was stilted when he huffed out, "Tracker."

Her eyes looked to Myles, her pretty brows furrowed.

"What tracker?" She asked.

He said nothing, then began laughing once again. Myles pressed in a bit firmer and his laugh changed to a howl.

"We have a tracker on him." His head motioned to him. Both Addy and Myles looked up at him slowly. Addy stood taller as their eyes locked together.

He felt helpless. He held his hands out to the side and shook his head.

Myles' eyes were murderous and to be honest, he couldn't blame him. Rafe had caused all sorts of trouble today. Not meaning to and certainly not trying to. But he'd brought the enemy not once, but twice.

"Where?" Myles ground out as he pushed in again.

The man coughed. After his coughing fit, Myles let up and the man gasped for air a couple of times then softly said, "We have trackers in his phone."

Myles glanced up at him. "We'll look as soon as we have this asshole secured."

Addy stepped away and pulled her phone from her back pocket. She stepped away far enough that she couldn't be heard. Myles continued to question the man.

"Who is paying you?"

The man's breathing grew ragged and Myles pushed into the wound once again. He howled, then nodded his head. Gathering his breath he finally said, "Warren Elliott."

"Who is that?"

"King's man."

"Man for what?"

The man began laughing. He sputtered out a cough, then laid his head back against the rails.

Myles glanced at him. "Start searching for Elliott."

The wounded man grunted and moaned slightly, but Myles didn't let up. Rafe turned and entered the cabin. Pulling his laptop out he logged into the system in the DoD. He typed in Warren Elliott.

The little wheel turned as the system worked through their data base. Finally, Warren Elliott's name appeared on the screen. Elliott's picture meant nothing to him. He'd never seen him before.

Reading his profile, he worked in the State Department, his position said, "Classified".

The door to the cabin opened and Addy entered. She glanced at the senator leaning back in the armchair, his eyes closed.

"How are you feeling Senator?"

His eyes opened slowly. His color was ashen. "I can't seem to catch my breath."

Addy neared him and laid her hand on his forehead. Lifting his hand, she pressed her fingers on his wrist and felt his pulse as she stared at her watch. Quickly striding toward her medical bag, she opened it and pulled a small white pill from a bottle.

Handing it to the senator, she pulled a bottle of water from a cooler and twisted the cap to open it.

"This is an aspirin. Please take it and drink a fair amount of water with it."

"What's that for? I don't have a headache."

"It's not for a headache."

She motioned toward the senator with the bottle of water and he slowly put the aspirin in his mouth and with shaking fingers, he took the water bottle from Addy and drank down the aspirin.

When he'd finished drinking, he held the water bottle out to her and Addy twisted the cap on and set the bottle on the side table next to the senator. "It's right here if you need more. I'm not leaving, so I'll be here to watch you."

The senator nodded slightly and laid back against the chair. The fear in his eyes was evident. His slow calculated moves were impossible to miss.

Addy strode toward him. Her features were soft and his heartbeat increased.

He stood as she neared and the instant she was in front of him, he bent and kissed her lips. Her lips kissed his in return and he pulled her close with his arms around her body. Her arms circled his waist and he deepened the kiss.

What

...moments before respond-
ing. When he did, his voice was gruff. "Watching you out
there, wrestling with that asshole..." His fingers softly
brushed the area the assailant had hit her. She saw his
throat constrict as he swallowed and the deep brown of
his eyes was impossible for her to look away from. "I realized something."

Her lips twitched slightly. "What did you realize?"

"I want to get to know you better. I want time with you.
I want you to be safe."

Her lips parted slightly and her eyes continued to
stare. Her heart beat so fast it was distracting. "I want to
get to know you better too."

He grinned, but she stepped back once more. She
whispered, "But, we have things to clean up here." She
motioned over her shoulder at the senator. "I think it's his
heart. We need to get him out of here. They'll come back.
And we need to get the tracker off your phone."

She held her hand out to him and her breathing came in spurts as she worried he would balk at the intrusion. But, to her surprise, he slowly laid his phone in her hand, never looking away from her.

His phone was warm in her hand. The weight of his similar to her own phone. She slid her finger over the screen and came to a password screen. She held it out to Rafe, and he easily entered his code and opened his phone.

She checked his texts, aware she was prying. Then, she plugged it into her laptop still sitting on the table. She tapped a few times in the GHOST system and began a search for the trojan horse that allowed King's men to enter their circle of security.

He had very few apps on his phone, which is where most trackers are located. Her computer alerted her to the calculator app on his phone. She tapped the keys to tell the program to search the calculator and watched as the circle turned.

A red box appeared on her screen and she read the location of the tracker. Tapping a few times she opened the calculator app and tapped into the settings. There it was, nestled quietly inside his calculator app.

Turning his phone toward him so he could see, his jaw tightened, and when his eyes met hers, they were no longer the velvety chocolate brown of before, but now his pupils dilated and his brows furrowed.

His voice was gruff when he asked, "Can you find a serial number or other identifier on the tracker?"

Myles entered the cabin and moved quickly toward them. "What have you found?"

She turned Rafe's phone toward Myles. His eyes

squinted briefly, then heaved out a deep breath. "It's a Sammasa fleet tracking app."

Rafe sat at the table and began typing into his computer. She focused on Myles. "How do we disable it?"

Myles pulled his laptop from the bag he'd stowed it in, opened the lid and immediately began typing. As he did that, she asked, "What did you do with the perp?"

"Henry's back. He's watching him."

A loud howl came from outside and Myles' lips turned up into a smile. "I guess he isn't cooperating."

Addy rolled her shoulders back. It went against the medic in her to continue to cause pain. But they needed answers.

Rafe huffed out a breath. "That is the app the State Department uses to track its government owned vehicles."

She looked at Rafe waiting for more of an explanation, but he wasn't offering anything further. Myles is the one who broke the silence. "How did it get in your phone?"

"I don't know."

Addy lay her right hand on Rafe's left shoulder. "Rafe, who has access to your phone?"

"No one."

"When Jensen Gable was in the locker room and put a tracker in your gym bag, could he have gotten into your phone?"

"There's no way. It's password locked and I can look at my phone data to see when it was last opened."

"Can you go back around the time you were at the gym, in the pool, to see if it was accessed?"

Myles interrupted. "According to this, the tracker was activated the day before that. Who had access to your phone two days ago?"

"That was the day the senator told Wade about the information he had on King." Rafe's fingers brushed across his forehead before digging into his hair and sweeping it off his forehead.

"I was in my office while the senator was in with Wade. I had my phone on my desk connected to the charger, which is also connected to my computer. I was in my office the entire time." He froze and his eyes rounded. "Except when Wade called me to his office after the senator left." He stood. "Shit!"

Myles questioned him further. "Who would have access to your office during the day and specifically during the time you were with Wade. Is there a way to tell?"

"I need to call my assistant."

Addy shook her head. "Could it be her?"

"It could be, but no one on the face of the earth would be more surprised than me. She's loyal and dependable. But, when I came back to my office that day, she mentioned the Distible documents on my desk. I don't know who put them there. She'll know."

Addy pulled a burner phone from the equipment duffle bag and handed it to Rafe. "You can use this. Myles needs to clean your phone."

Rafe took the phone from her. Heat rose up her arm when their fingers touched. She let out a long breath as he dialed the number to his assistant. She shouldn't be thinking about him as a man right now when there was so much on the line.

"Leesha, who put the Distible documents on my desk a few days ago?" He brushed his fingers through his dark hair again. She liked when he did that. His hair looked silky the way it fell over his forehead when his fingers brushed through it.

"It's important." He offered. "You're sure?"

His chest rose and fell and his lips turned down into a frown. "Thank you, Leesha."

He hung up the phone and sat at his computer again.

up at her

office. He brought the documents into my office while I was in Wade's office. He's the only person who had access to my phone at that time."

Addy nodded then turned to Myles. "How long does it take to install a tracker like that?"

"A couple of minutes if you know what you're doing."

Rafe didn't even look up as he kept typing. "I'm researching Brett Selisen right now."

Addy's phone rang and she stepped away to answer it. He half listened, half watched the information on Brett Selisen populate on his computer. Former military, he'd served two years in the Army before honorable medical discharge.

Rafe dug further into Brett Selisen. Their private server had compiled documents on every employee who worked with them. Wade was thorough. Brett Selisen had amassed some hefty medical bills. Rafe heaved out a heavy breath then clicked into the banking information portal. He typed in Brett's name and watched his bank records populate.

His head slowly nodded as the evidence presented itself. "Brett Selisen received a large deposit of money from an overseas account the day the senator spoke with Wade."

Addy appeared from the kitchen area. "Tate has a new place for the senator and the documents. Myles and Henry are taking him back to Glen Hollow. I'm staying here until we find out where Brett Selisen is and who hired him."

Myles stood, set Rafe's phone on the table next to his laptop and nodded to him. "It's clean."

Myles then turned to Addy. "Are you sure you won't need backup?"

"I might, but I'll have to rely on Rafe. You and Henry may encounter trouble along the way back to Glen Hollow. The plane will be at the airport in two hours. In the meantime, we need to get out of here."

"What about the perp?" Myles asked.

"Tate will have someone come and get him and the body."

Addy turned to him. "Rafe, help us pack everything up."

Rafe stood and tucked his laptop into its case. He pocketed his cell phone then started rolling up cords with Myles. He felt all of this deep in his gut. His stomach felt soured and he vowed to himself to make all of this up to Addy. And the rest of them, but mostly to her. Twice now, because of him, they had to pack up abruptly and move. As soon as he and Addy were safe, he'd fall down the rabbit hole of finding Brett Selisen and getting to the bottom of who he worked for. Then, Brett would be let go and he'd brainstorm with Wade on periodic checkups on anyone working with them.

He carried totes and duffle bags to the various vehicles. He and Addy would keep half of the equipment and Myles and Henry would keep the other half.

Once they'd packed everything up, Henry and Myles helped the senator to his car. "What about my family?" The senator whined.

Henry responded, "We're looking for them and plan on keeping them safe."

"We have a place in Hawaii. They may have gone there."

"Why the fuck didn't you tell us that before?" Henry boomed.

The senator started blustering on about something else but Henry closed the car door on him.

Addy strode to the vehicle and punched fists with Henry. "Stay safe, keep your eyes peeled. Tell Everleigh I said hi. Get the senator medical attention as soon as you get back."

His grin was broad when Everleigh's name was mentioned and Rafe felt a little pang of jealousy at the obvious smitten look on Henry's face. He loved his wife. He had a someone. A person.

Myles put the last duffle in the trunk of the car and turned to Addy. She hugged him. "Tell Maya I'll call as soon as I can. You guys take care."

Myles nodded. "Will do. You stay safe. Things have been bumpy."

"It's not intentional and now that we've figured it out, it should be good."

Myles glanced over Addy's head at him and nodded but said nothing else. He turned and got into the passenger seat of the vehicle and Henry waved out the window as they pulled away from the cabin.

Addy turned to him. "Ready?"

"Yes."

The perp whined, "Hey, what the fuck? You're leaving me here?"

Addy glanced at him. "Someone's coming for you."

Just as the words were out of her mouth, a vehicle pulled into the driveway. Addy stared at the vehicle for a long time, then quietly said, "It's ours."

"How do you know?"

"The tags. Tate gave me the tag number."

"Okay."

She started toward their SUV. "Let's go. They'll likely not want to be seen in person."

He followed her to the SUV they'd brought here, a slight grin on his face when she walked around to the passenger side and slid inside. He jumped into the driver's seat and started the SUV. He immediately began moving toward the road, only one brief glance in the mirror to see the two men striding toward the man zip-tied to the porch.

"Do I want to know what they'll do to him?"

Addy turned to him, a beautiful smile on her face. "We're not animals, Rafe. They'll take him in for medical attention then they'll question the hell out of him. His friend will be taken care of."

"How?"

She shook her beautiful head. "Don't ask too many questions."

He nodded then let out a deep breath. "I have some things to tell you. Are you ready for that conversation?"

"Is it about getting to know me better?"

"Yes. No. A little of both I guess."

She swallowed and sat back in her seat. "Okay. Go ahead."

Rafe's heart hammered in his chest. It was the first time he was saying it out loud. He'd kept the secret for years. "Wade is Casper."

Her head slowly turned toward him. She said nothing but her body tensed and she was alert and waiting for more. "He's training me to be his replacement."

"You're serious?"

"I am."

"Why are you telling me? You said you had to keep secrets."

"Wade told me this was too serious to keep the secret any longer and that it would likely come out to GHOST anyway. He was on the track to retirement just before the senator came to see him. I've been working for Wade for ten years. He's been training me for the last three."

Addy sat back in her seat and stared out the windshield. Her full lips hung open and he saw her heartbeat in her neck. He navigated a corner onto a county road that would soon merge off onto the highway. She didn't say anything for so long he worried this was bad news.

"I take it we're going to the Bowman home?" He finally asked.

She whispered, "Yes."

Roxanne had this time he'd had never said anything about Wade being Casper. Even after Roxanne and Hawk married. Maybe she didn't know. But, now that Addy knew, she had to tell Tate. He could tell his dad, Gaige. That would likely create a silence in the building like they had in this vehicle now. What did you say to something like that?

"I'd appreciate it if you'd say something." His deep voice broke the silence.

She turned to face him again. "I'm speechless I guess. We never tried to find out who Casper was. It didn't matter and we felt he had a reason for staying hidden. He's always been good to our firm and each of us. I'm shocked to hear this. And, now you're going to be the new Casper? Why are you telling me that?"

"Wade wanted it out in the open with all of you. Since his family has now been threatened, he's worried our silence will get some of us hurt or killed. And his identity was hidden for all these years because his job at the DoD would be compromised. I'm sure the DoD wouldn't appreciate knowing the Secretary of Defense hired special operatives to do the work the DoD should be doing. There are rules and laws. All of which have been broken."

She swallowed the enormous lump in her throat. "Do you want this? To be Casper? It's against the policy of your job, isn't it?"

"But it's for the greater good. What you all do, is what the military and police can't do, because of some of the stupidest regulations and laws. There shouldn't be a gap between the two entities and yet there is. Good people get caught in that gap. It's against Wade's moral compass to let them perish because of it. That's why he got involved in the first place. Before GHOST he had another group who ceased to exist about a year after GHOST was formed. He...We need you. You need us. And the people caught in the middle need both of us."

Addy sat back and digested this explanation. He was right, of course. The people caught in the middle needed someone to help them.

"I agree."

She blew out a breath as Rafe turned the SUV onto the street behind the Bowman home. She pulled her phone up and texted Catalina to notify her they were coming home. After what she'd been through earlier, surprises weren't likely welcome.

As they approached the garage behind the home, the door began to open and Addy smiled. Catalina.

Rafe pulled the SUV into the garage next to his vehicle. She saw him grimace after looking at his vehicle and she chuckled. "It's all good now."

He shook his head. "It's not good. I'm happy it's rectified, but good is not how I'd describe it."

She shrugged. "Suit yourself. There was no way you could have known about the tracker or the app. We've neutralized both of them and now we move on."

"If I'm to replace Casper, I can't have things like that happen."

She stared at him for a long time, he looked sad. "Maybe you should ask Casper if anything like that ever happened to him. I don't think there is a perfect human being out there. And, criminals are criminals, even if they work in your office."

He stepped out of the vehicle and rather than wait for him to walk around, she jumped out and moved toward the door. He grabbed her hand as she passed him. A tug of her arm had her pressed tightly to the front of his body. His left hand rested against the back of her head. Her face turned up to look into his handsome face. The look in his eyes took her breath away. It was a look she hadn't seen on him before. And with their bodies pressed tightly together as they were, she felt the desire grow between them.

He bent down. She rose up. Their lips pressed together perfectly. His were soft and pliant, she hoped hers were too. His right arm snaked around her waist and pulled her to him tightly. She raised her arms and wrapped them around his neck, enjoying the way her breasts felt pushed tightly against his t-shirt clad chest. He was firm and muscular, the ridges of his muscles pressed against her were exciting.

His tongue slid sensually along her lips. She opened her lips and embraced the feel of his tongue as it seductively slid along hers. Slow. Wet. Soft. Passionate kisses were her kryptonite.

His arms loosened around her body and she felt a loss. When their lips parted, his kissed her forehead so tenderly it was as if a butterfly wing had touched her. Opening her eyes, she saw him watching her. They stared deep as if he were trying to see her soul. To read her thoughts. To dig so deep inside of her he'd never leave. And she liked it.

She inhaled but when she let that breath out, it was shaky. There was no hiding that emotion.

His beautiful lips parted slightly, then turned up at the corners. "I feel the same way about you. I honestly haven't felt this way about another human my entire life. You're different in a good way Adelaide Masters."

She swallowed and tried deep breathing again. "Yeah." She stepped back. "I haven't felt this way about anyone in my life either. It makes me mad to be honest, because it confuses me. I need to focus right now and I'm struggling with that because of you."

It was his turn to take a deep, shaky breath. He nodded his handsome head, took her hand in his, and led her to the service door at the side of the garage. "I guess it's good we both feel this way. At least there won't be the worry that the other doesn't feel the same."

"I guess." She mumbled.

He chuckled. "Let's go do our jobs at the highest level we can and get to know each other better at the same time. I've known of you for a long time Addy. I've read all of Casper's reports. I've been impressed with you from the beginning. I'm not wrong."

They marched across the back lawn to the kitchen door. "You have me at a disadvantage. I didn't know anything about you until a few days ago."

aromas that made his stomach

Addy glanced back at him and grinned. "Wait till you taste Catalina's cooking."

"I'm ready. We haven't eaten much today."

A woman was cutting up vegetables on an old wooden cutting board on the counter. When she turned, she had a knife in her hand. Rafe's eyes went to the knife, then to her face. She saw that and turned and set the knife on the cutting board. Not that he thought someone cooking was there to kill them.

When she turned again to face them, her cheeks had turned pink.

Addy chuckled. "Catalina, you remember Rafe Martin. Rafe, not sure if you formally met Catalina."

He stepped around Addy and held his hand out to Catalina. She brusquely wiped her hands on the towel she had hanging from her waist. Her dark hair had graying strands interspersed which caught the over-head lights in the kitchen and sparkled.

"It's nice to meet you, formerly, Catalina. I understand you run the household."

Catalina's cheeks reddened. "No sir. I am only here for the Bowman family. To be honest, Miss Roxanne runs the house. I only do her bidding. Happily. She is easy to work for."

Addy chuckled. "Roxanne is very nice." She turned to Rafe. "Roxanne is Henry's mother. This is her family home, as you likely already know. But, I don't want to assume, so..."

His chuckle came deep from his chest. "Thank you for not assuming. I am aware, but don't mind the reminder."

Addy nodded to Catalina. "It's just Rafe and I here now Catalina. Henry and Myles had to go home."

The smile faded from Catalina's face. "Yes. Miss Roxanne called and told me. I am sorry I didn't get to say goodbye to Mr. Henry."

Addy grinned and it was adorable. "He'll be back."

Catalina nodded and wiped her hands once again. "Okay. I need to change sheets in the bedrooms for Mr. Martin. Which room will you prefer?"

Rafe offered Catalina his brightest smile. "We'll figure it out. Please don't bother for me. Honestly, I'm former military, I've slept on used sheets more times than I can count."

That seemed to make Catalina nervous. She stepped back and mumbled, "I'll change them all. I don't want Miss Roxanne to think I am not treating her guests well."

Before he could reassure her, she scampered out of the room and disappeared. Addy turned to him, a pretty grin on her face. "You're too handsome for most women. We need to get to work. We've mostly set up operations in the dining room because there were more of us than desks in the office, but now, we can move operations to the office and stay out of Catalina's way when she's trying to set the table for dinner. It's right this way."

He remembered seeing the office when he'd visited a couple of days ago, but didn't mind following Addy. Her backside was most intriguing to watch as she moved. Each little cheek taking turns moving up then down with her footsteps. They walked under the grand staircase, then entered the foyer to the living room which was to the right, the office to the left. He followed Addy to the left.

The office was elegant in its styling. Deep gray walls and white painted woodwork trimmed the floor, windows, and bookcases. The desks were of old wood engraved styling but painted white. The desks were identical except one was smaller than the other, but they sat directly across the room and faced each other. The larger one to the left, the smaller to the right.

Addy pointed to the larger desk to the left, "Why don't you take that one?"

He stared into her eyes. "This may seem old-fashioned, but that looks like the desk the man of the house would use. I'm not the man of the house and I'm not running this operation. You are."

She shrugged. "That is old-fashioned, I guess. But, I'm only running this mission, not the entire operation, that task falls to Tate. And the smaller desk fits my size better than the larger one."

He grinned. "I guess it does. This space is beautiful."

Addy moved to the long windows directly across from the entrance to the office and turned to him. "This entire home is beautiful. Roxanne had it redone a few years ago.

She said it made her sad to see her parents' desks still sitting exactly as they had been when they died. She'd kept them like that for years, but felt it was time. From what I understand, these are the original desks, she just had them painted. She's managed to update most of the rooms over the years. I remember them coming here when Henry and Stella were little. We all hated when they were gone because we enjoyed them so much. But, every time they came back, it was like Christmas all over again. We felt like that about each of us when we were gone." She smiled at her memories, and it left him with a hard pit in his stomach.

He swallowed. "I'm glad you have all those good memories and friends from your childhood."

She cocked her head to the right as her eyes bored into his. "Don't you have good memories from your childhood? Or friends?"

Usually when this question came around while dating, or getting to know someone of the opposite sex, he'd change the subject. Instead, he took a deep breath and shook his head. "Not really. I have a brother and sister, whom I love very much. But our childhoods were more about staying out of our parents' way and not getting sucked into the shit they both stirred up in town."

He waited for the judgment. His heart thumped in his chest and his throat dried out. Instead, Addy stepped toward him. She placed her hands on either side of his waist. She stood on her toes and softly kissed his lips. "I'm sorry." She whispered. "I can't take it away, but then again, it's what made you who you are today, so I wouldn't want to."

His eyes misted and he blinked rapidly then closed

them tightly as he pulled her to him. The sucker punch of emotion her comment gave him had his head swirling.

Footsteps behind them made her pull away slightly. He twisted to see Catalina come down the staircase with an armful of sheets in her arms. She didn't look into the office, though she likely knew they were there. She disappeared around the staircase, and he sucked in a lungful of air.

"Okay. I need to locate Brett Selisen and you need to contact Tate."

handsome

shirt and dress pants. He was going to go to his place later today so he could get a couple changes of clothing. She'd never said anything about him staying here, he never asked. It was assumed. That was kind of nice. It meant he wanted to stay here with her. It also, hopefully, meant they'd be together. It had been a long time since she'd felt the desire to be with someone special. It actually felt like a lifetime. And, as she thought on it now, she'd never felt like this about anyone in her past.

Letting out a deep breath, she picked up her phone and tapped Tate's picture. She stared across the room at Rafe. He glanced at her periodically and she got goose-bumps every time. When his lips curved up into a half smile, she liked that more.

"Hey, Addy, what's up?"

She sat straighter in her chair. "I have something to tell you."

"Okay. Have you found Jensen Gable?"

His question took her back a moment, she'd been so focused on telling him about Casper, and Rafe. "Ah, no. That's next on my list actually."

"Okay."

"Tate. Casper is Wade Evans. Rafe Martin, his Special Counsel, is being groomed to take over for Casper when he retires."

Tate's chair squeaked and she imagined him sitting in it. His voice was monotone when he responded. "How do you know this?"

"Rafe told me. Casper told him it was too dangerous keeping the secret from us."

"Okay." He took a deep breath. "It actually makes sense to many things now."

"Yeah. Have you gotten to his family?"

"Yes. Wyatt and Axel are bringing them back to Indiana. Casper is still dark."

"Rafe has access to him."

"Shit." She heard the squeak once again. "I need to talk to him."

She stood and padded across the plush carpeting in the office. Rafe looked up at her as she approached and sat back in his chair. His eyes never left hers as she rounded the desk, tapped her phone and set it on the desk, between Rafe's computer and her hip.

"Tate, I have you on speaker. Rafe is here. Rafe, meet Tate."

Rafe grinned. "It's nice to meet you, Tate."

"It's nice to meet you too, Rafe. So, Addy tells me you have access to Casper."

"I do."

"I need to speak to him. Wyatt and Axel have his wife

and kids and are bringing them to GHOST Headquarters in Indiana. They'll be safe there. We'd like Casper to join them there so he's safe as well."

"He's working on getting the information the senator shared with him into the correct hands before the inauguration."

"I understand. We can help him with that. It's dangerous, as you've witnessed."

"Yes. King won't go down without a war."

"That's my worry. Is it worth it?"

Rafe's brows furrowed tightly in his forehead and he sat up straight. She saw his jaw twitch before he said, "Is having a corrupt president the right thing? The people only elected him because they didn't know all the dirt on him. Is that fair? Is that right? And, if he'll have someone killed to keep them quiet, and not only one person, but many, is that the person who should lead our country?"

Tate sucked in a deep breath and let it out before answering. "Casper chose wisely."

Rafe's jaw twitched again, but his shoulders relaxed. "I'll ask him to contact you Tate."

"Thank you. Addy, I have a few more things for you."

She picked up her phone, tapped the speaker off, and put it to her ear. She stared at Rafe a moment, he never looked away from her. They were in this together, and it felt right. She trusted he'd do anything he could to watch her back and she'd do the same. That felt good. He had honor, and values. All the things her parents taught her to value.

She grinned then padded across the floor to her desk and sat. But Rafe still watched her, and she found it impossible to look away from him.

"Okay. What else do you need Tate?"

"Upload your report on the two assailants. Then, we need to find Jensen Gable. And, the red-haired man in the bar the first night, I think he's the main henchman. The senator thinks his name is Brett or something."

She sat up straight in her chair and stared across the room at Rafe. "Brett Selisen?"

"The senator didn't know his last name. Why do you know that name?"

"Brett Selisen is an aide in Rafe's office and the person we believe planted the tracker in Rafe's phone."

Tate's chair squeaked again, but her eyes never looked away from Rafe's.

Tate's fingers flew over his keyboard, the tapping sound was unmistakable. She could see him furiously searching. "Okay. We need to find Brett Selisen."

"Rafe's working on that now."

"Okay. Talk later." Tate ended the call and before she could say anything Rafe's phone rang.

He moved woodenly as he lifted his phone to his ear. Their eyes locked as if unable to look away.

"Rafe Martin."

He listened for a few moments, then his spine stiffened. "When was this?"

"I'll be right there."

He ended the call and stood from the desk. "My house was broken into an hour ago."

She shot up from her chair, already moving toward the office door. "Did they catch anyone there?"

"No. The police are dusting for fingerprints now. But I suspect if the burglar was sent by King's men, there will be none."

"Were any other homes broken into?"

"Just mine."

[illegible] stepped. [illegible] Especially if [illegible]

"How long have you lived here?"

"About five years."

Addy let a whoosh of air from her lungs. "You said it had security at the gates and you have cameras."

"Yes. My camera alerts didn't go off. Security was [illegible]"

"Selisen could have shut your notifications off on your phone when he accessed it to add the tracker. As to the security here, what do they have at the gate?"

"A guard. Cameras at all entrances and exits."

His eyes scanned the area as he turned into the main entrance. There were police cruisers flanking the entrance, red and blue lights flashing. The guard who normally worked the gate was sitting on a stool, just outside the guard house, the small enclosure to keep him out of inclement weather. He shook his head as he spoke to police, clearly he was distraught and likely worried he'd be out of a job.

Rafe slowed his SUV and rolled the window down. An officer approached the vehicle and Rafe held his ID Badge up for him to see.

"Hi, Officer. I'm Rafe Martin. It's my house that was broken into."

The officer looked at the badge, then at him. He paused for a few moments, then nodded. "You can go in Mr. Martin. I'll radio ahead and let officers on the scene know you're on your way."

Rafe nodded and slowly pulled forward between the gates. He swallowed the lump in his throat. The betrayals and violations just kept coming.

He glanced briefly at Addy, who stared out the windshield looking for anything that seemed off. Though, honestly, she'd never been here, so how would she know, unless it was obvious.

He turned onto his street and the police vehicles had blocked his home from both sides. Lights flashed and he assumed his neighbors were rather irritated. And, likely nervous too. They felt so secure in this neighborhood. As if this was the safest place on earth. Of course, a person would like to feel that way about their home.

He pulled to the side of the street and put his vehicle in park. He shut it off and looked over at Addy. "You can stay here if you like."

She smiled and it was just what he needed. "I'll come with you."

She opened her door before he opened his and he knew she wouldn't wait for him to help her down from the vehicle, but he could take her hand and walk her in.

He moved swiftly to her side of the vehicle and took

her hand in his. He squeezed as they neared his home, more to reassure himself than her. He, for the most part, vacillated between being angry and being scared. He'd spent plenty of time and money getting his house the way he liked it and the first time Addy saw it, he hoped it wasn't trashed.

An officer approached them as they moved across the front lawn. "Officer, I'm Rafe Martin. This is my house."

"Mr. Martin, we're glad to see you're alive and well. With all the blood we weren't sure of the condition we'd find you in."

"Blood?" His heart raced and the thrumming in his ears nearly drowned everything else out. "What blood?"

The officer stepped back and motioned toward the house. "You should go in and see for yourself Mr. Martin."

He tightened his hold on Addy's hand then stepped toward the house, dread filling his stomach with each step.

He moved through the entrance first, not caring that he wasn't being gentlemanly. Not sure what they would see, he felt it should be him first in this instance.

Inside, the foyer and living area looked just as he'd left it. Nothing much seemed out of place. His steps were slow and deliberate as he moved into the living room. The fireplace he so appreciated looked straight and tall as it had when he'd last been here. The pictures of Brent and Brooke were right where he'd left them. No blood to be found.

Moving to the right, the kitchen lights were all on, and officers stepped through the room. Fingerprint dust was on the hard surfaces. The counters, the refrigerator, the oven, the microwave, and his coffee maker. The floor also had a few spots where fingerprint dust had been taped off.

He thought it was weird there'd be fingerprints on the tile floors.

An officer nodded to him. "Chief is in the office, Mr. Martin."

Rafe nodded and pulled Addy to the office with him. His throat dried out and he had that eerie feeling one gets just before bad news is heard. Stepping into the office, he saw three police officers snapping pictures, dusting for prints and taking samples from the desk, the credenza, and his bookshelves.

"Mr. Martin. I'm Chief Mueller. Do you have any idea where all this blood came from?"

"No." He sounded like he was in a tunnel. His own voice sounded far away. "Whose is it?"

"We were hoping you'd be able to shed some light on that for us."

"I can't. I don't know what the blood came from. I also don't know who came into my home. How were you notified that my home had been breached?"

"We received a call at the station."

"From who?"

"We don't know. I only know a call came in that someone was in the house and there was a lot of yelling then a man, who looked similar to you, ran out the back door and ducked between the neighbors' yards and ran down the back street."

"What time was that?"

The chief flipped open his notebook and read down the small page of his scribbles. "It seems that was about two o'clock this afternoon."

"So, someone broke into my house at just before two this afternoon, created a damned mess, ran out into the backyard and between the neighbors' yards and down the street and you think that was me? If I were going to do something like this, don't you think I'd wait until the dead of the night?"

"I'm not accusing you Mr. Martin."

Rafe turned his head and saw the mess. Addy squeezed his hand. "Chief. Rafe was with me and my teammates all morning and afternoon. When the call came in that his home had been broken into, we were at the home of Raymond and Kate Bowman, now owned by their children. The housekeeper was there and can attest to that fact should you need her too."

The chief looked at Addy, then in his eyes for a long cold stare. "I haven't accused either of you of doing anything. I don't know why you'd jump to needing someone to 'attest' to your whereabouts."

She smiled her prettiest smile. "I simply wanted you to know, we have been otherwise occupied all day and have witnesses. We also wouldn't come to Rafe's home, the one you can tell is pristine and cleaned, at least it was, to cause someone harm, smear it about the place, then run and call the police to implicate ourselves."

Rafe squeezed her hand again, his brain finally engaging. "Chief, I'd like to see all the reports as soon as you have them typed up. Including who called in the supposed burglary or intrusion. Who saw the man who looked like me, running across the yard and the identifying features of this man. I'd like the fingerprint reports, the blood analysis, and every single interview you've conducted here this afternoon."

"I don't believe you have the authority Mr. Martin."

"Oh, but I do." Rafe pulled out his DoD security, and showed it to the chief, then he finished, "Anything to do with a DoD employee, especially the employees surrounding the Secretary of Defense, are subject to immediate investigation by the Department. And, as we're currently involved in something that has to do with national security, I'll have those reports immediately upon completion, which should be within the hour."

mind of Rafe

change like he'd

grinned, then he proceeded to the door, still holding her hand and bringing her along. He said nothing as he moved to his bedroom. He flicked the light on and led her to an armchair in the corner.

"If you don't mind, please take a seat while I pack a few things."

"I can help."

He grinned. "They're going to give me a hard time about packing clothing. I want you to sit there, while I lay a few things out on the bed. I'm going to invite one of the officers to watch so there isn't an issue later on. It'll look better if you are sitting there and not milling about."

She sat in the comfortable chair, excited 'in charge' Rafe was back in action. He hadn't completely disappeared, but he'd certainly taken a backseat the past day.

Rafe disappeared from the room for a few moments and she took the time to look around. He had great taste in furniture. His bedroom was masculine, but not overly so. The bed was large, easily a king-size bed with a deep brown suede duvet. Plush pillows graced the head of the bed, the large, padded leather headboard filled nearly half the wall behind the bed. This leather chair she sat in was soft to the touch and comfortable to sit in. Behind her an oversized crocheted gray blanket was draped prettily over the back. The dark wooden dresser held only a wood and metal wallet organizer, and she could see some change laying in the tray. The carpet was neutral in color and soft to walk on. Little expense was spared in making this room exactly what he wanted.

Rafe entered the room with one of the officers from the kitchen in tow. He glanced at her when he entered, then winked. Damn that did all sorts of good things to her body, but she simply smiled at him then nodded at the officer. Rafe stepped to his closet and slid the barn door open to reveal neatly arranged shelves with sweaters, t-shirts, and work out clothing neatly folded and gracing their appropriate shelves. He stepped aside and held his hand out to the officer.

"My suitcase is standing near the shelves. I'll be filling it with clothing."

The officer nodded. His eyes darted to hers often, and she simply smiled at him and tried to act relaxed. What she got was that Rafe was pissed off. They'd accused him of doing something to his own home, planting blood and wasting their time. His way of handling it was he was going to be a pain in the ass. If not a bit of a smart-ass.

He pulled the suitcase out and opened it on the bed. He nodded to the officer and turned to pull underwear and t-shirts from his drawers. He plopped the undergarments on the bed near the suitcase, then moved to the closet. He pulled three pair of khakis from hangers and set them on the bed. He returned the hangers to the end of the closet rod and pulled clean shirts, sweaters, and workout clothing from the closet and placed them on his bed. He stepped into a room next to his closet, which she guessed was his bathroom. He came out with a toiletry bag and laid that on the bed.

He strutted to the bedside table and pulled his charging stand and the cord off of it, then wrapped the cord neatly into a figure eight pattern, secured it with the Velcro attached to it and laid it near his clothing on the bed. He then looked at the officer, his chest rising and falling from the pace he'd set.

"Any objection to me packing this stuff?"

"No sir." The officer softly replied.

Rafe nodded and began neatly placing his items into the suitcase. When he'd finished, he zipped it closed, set it on the floor, wheels down and lifted the handle. "Anything you need from me before we go?"

The officer shook his head. "No, sir."

He turned his handsome head to her, smiled slightly, though it didn't reach his eyes. "Are you ready, Addy?"

"Yes." She replied as she stood. She offered the officer a smile. Mostly she felt sorry for him. He had to stand there and watch Rafe pack, knowing full well Rafe was pissed off. Also knowing, Rafe had done nothing wrong.

Rafe moved toward his front door, his back straight as an arrow, his jaw clenching as he walked. The officers fingerprinting the kitchen didn't look at them as they left and she was grateful for that. He'd likely snap their heads off.

As he stepped onto the front patio, he let out a deep breath and she placed her hand in his once more.

"It's fine. I'll be fine. We'll do whatever we have to do to make sure you're safe."

When he replied, his jaw was tight. "I'm not worried about being safe. I'm worried about the magnitude this shit show will bend to. It looks like they're trying to frame me."

"Shouldn't we stay and make sure they don't?"

"No. We're going to find Brett Selisen. I'm going to bet he's behind this."

They hurried along the lawn to Rafe's SUV. He stuffed his suitcase in the backseat, then turned to her. He opened the door and pulled her toward the SUV and his body. He bent his head down, kissed her lips lightly then helped her into the vehicle.

She buckled herself in as he strode around the front of the vehicle. As soon as he slid into the driver's seat, he pulled up his phone. He recalled his security system, then scrolled through the videos that it had taken that day. He leaned over toward her, his phone out so she could see it, and tapped on a video with the time stamp 2:03 p.m.

The video began playing and she watched as a man approached the house. He knocked on the front door, then rang the doorbell. He looked both ways down the street then pulled something from his pocket and opened the door.

"Is there a way he got a key?"

Rafe shook his head. "I don't use that door on a regular basis, so I wouldn't have had keys at the office. I pull into the garage and come in the back door which is attached to the garage. He used the front door, not the garage service door."

She nodded and continued to watch the man. After he disappeared into the house, the security system failed to log anything else. Rafe, then looked at the next video, which triggered at 2:27 p.m. "He was in the house for only twenty-four minutes."

The man exited the back door into the backyard. He jogged across the lawn, turned back to the house, that's when the hood on his sweatshirt dropped down and the red hair showed. She sucked in her breath. "That's the man from the bar the other night. The one that scared the senator. He came in and watched us for a while, then he followed the senator out the back door. But Henry went with the senator, so nothing happened."

Rafe pulled up the settings from his security system and turned his phone toward her. "My notifications were turned off."

Rafe dropped his hand to his lap. "That man is Brett Selisen."

Addy picked up her phone and dialed Tate. When he answered she quickly asked, "Tate. Can you find out what time a call was made to the police department in Arlington to come to Rafe's house? We're here now, it's swarming with police. He was told a call came in to the police that his house had been burglarized. There is security at the gate to get into this neighborhood and I can't figure out who would have called. No one would know there'd been a burglary at all. It appears Rafe's being set up."

"Hang tight, let me see what I can find out. I'll call you right back."

"Thanks."

She ended the call.

Rafe then used his phone. "I'm calling Wade."

eyes were invaded his house, and the thing that was most was that there was little urgency in their movements. They sauntered around as if this was a coffee break.

"Rafe, what's happening?"

"Wade, I have Addy here and we're on speaker."

"Hello, Addy."

"Hello, Wade."

"What do you have going on there? I've got some interesting movement on my computer."

Rafe nodded and swallowed to moisten his throat. "I think I'm being set up for something. My house was broken into. It was Brett Selisen, though the police don't know that. At least not from me. I saw him on my camera. Blood was smeared in my home office and from what I can tell, not much more was moved or touched. Other than the fingerprint dust all over, it seemed as though things were in place. The office, some of the drawers had been pulled open, but nothing was tossed."

"Okay. Let me see if I can find anything out about that here. I'm listening to the chatter on the police radios and I've got someone inside King's office now."

"Police let me and Addy enter the house, grab a suitcase full of clothes and leave. They didn't ask me to look around and see if anything was missing. They didn't ask me much of anything. All they made comments about was that the man looked like me who left my home. Brett Selisen has reddish hair and is about five inches shorter than I am, and about thirty pounds heavier. So, it would be hard to mistake him for me."

"Do you know anything about the blood?"

"Not yet. I demanded the reports as soon as they came in. I don't know if they'll comply. If King has them on payroll already, he wants to scare me because he knows the senator shared secrets with you. He may think I'll lead them to you."

"I'm on my way out of town right now. You know where I'll be. If it gets too hot in D.C. you need to get out. Do you hear me? We need you safe. They won't want you to leave if they find out what we're doing."

He glanced at Addy. She stared into his eyes and her lips relaxed into a soft smile. "We'll be safe."

"Addy, I know you don't want to hear this, but if things go south, you let Rafe guard you from it. I owe your parents a great deal for years of service. I'd never want anything to happen to you on my watch."

Her lips stretched into a straight line. "I'll promise to be careful and work with Rafe. We'll guard each other."

Wade huffed out a deep breath. "Fair enough."

Rafe brushed Addy's cheek with the back of his

fingers. Then Wade continued. "I'll let you know as soon as I have anything. You'll have safety at the Bowman home. Use the safe room if anyone tries to get inside."

"Roger."

The line went silent. Rafe sat up straight and started his vehicle. "In case they think they're going to drag me to jail tonight, let's get out of here."

"Okay."

Rafe's phone signaled a text. It was from Wade.

"Guarding Adelaide is priority one. I've got
a way to get the information about King in
the proper hands. Stay safe."

After reading his text, he slid his phone into the cupholder in his vehicle and made a U-turn on his street. He moved down the street slowly, watching each house as he passed. Neighbors weren't looking out the windows, and many of the houses still looked empty. He glanced at his dashboard and saw the time was four-thirty-five. It was a bit early for Washington folks.

"Who would call the police anyway? No one is home during the day here. Everyone works." He mumbled.

Addy's phone rang as Rafe merged them onto the highway. "Hi, Tate. I have you on speaker. Rafe and I are in the car headed back to the Bowmans' house."

"Hi, Rafe." She could hear typing and knew he was still looking at things on his computer. "It looks like there was a little break in at the morgue today. I had the body Myles downed taken there secretly. We have a guy there who will put folks on ice until we figure out what to do with them. He phoned me to tell me the body brought in today is missing. I'm going to guess, they've planted his blood in your house Rafe, and they'll try to pin his murder on you.

At a minimum, they'll use it to squeeze you to get to Wade."

Rafe took a deep breath and let it out slowly. "We need to find Brett Selisen. I think I can find out where he is."

"Approaching him is dangerous. Use all precaution."

Addy nodded. "Will do. If we need to get out of the state, can the plane be on standby for us?"

"I'll have Gavin fly in and be at the private hanger we have there."

"Thanks, Tate."

"Rafe. I know this isn't your usual gig, so if you want to tap out, just let Addy know."

Rafe looked at Addy. She had a big grin on her face. "I'm good. I haven't worked in this capacity for a long time, but it's just like riding a bike."

The call ended.

Rafe left the highway and turned into the Bowman neighborhood. He glanced back often to make sure they weren't followed.

Addy twisted in her seat. "They know we're staying here. Selisen or someone was here earlier."

"Correct. Why don't we run in, grab your things, tell Catalina to go home, and go to a hotel."

32

They're likely

I'll text Catalina and

I don't want her traumatized again

Once she's safely away, we'll park a couple of streets over and sneak in through the back. Most of our equipment can be picked up later. I'll grab my clothing. My laptop is always with me and here in the vehicle."

"Please go home. The house is likely being watched, if you want a police escort, let me know."

She saw the dots bouncing and waited. Rafe drove them slowly around the outside of the neighborhood.

"My husband is here and we'll go home together."

"Let me know when you're safely out of the house."

She watched out the windshield as Rafe crawled the neighborhood. She turned her head toward him. "I almost forgot, there's a secret tunnel from the basement to the garage. If we can slip into the garage and get the door down before anyone sees us, we can get into the house that way."

"I haven't seen a single vehicle on the streets or in driveways. If they're watching it's from inside a house."

"That's perfect. The street the garage is on, is bordered by tall cedars on all sides. No one will see us pull into the garage."

Rafe drove the vehicle down the street then turned on the backstreet that led to the Bowman garage. They both watched diligently for any out-of-place vehicle, any person watching. "It looks clear."

Her phone buzzed a text.

"We're out of the house and neighborhood."

"Catalina is gone."

He pushed the garage door button hanging on the visor and approached the garage slowly.

Turning the SUV into the garage, he hit the button to close the door instantly and they sat still inside until the door shut.

Addy jumped from the vehicle and moved to the front of the garage. She located the tunnel entrance near the wall, now covered by a heavy rubber mat. She lifted the mat, and Rafe pulled it over to expose the tunnel door. A keypad lock had been installed a few years ago. Addy lifted the metal keypad cover and typed in the code. She closed the cover then opened the cover to the handle and twisted it to unlock the door. She lifted the metal door in the floor and Rafe whistled lightly. "That is seriously cool."

She grinned. "When Hawk met Roxanne, she escaped out this door to get away from him. He caught her though."

"I'd love to have seen that."

She chuckled, then lowered herself into the hole in the ground, using the metal ring steps in the side of it. She felt the wall for the light switch and turned the lights on in the tunnel. Waiting at the bottom for Rafe, she whispered up to him., "Close the hatch, in case they breech the garage."

He reached up and pulled the door closed, then hustled down the metal steps to her. Addy moved toward the basement slowly, trying to listen for sounds. Rafe followed closely behind.

As they neared the end of the tunnel, she stopped and listened. She didn't hear anything and slowly opened the door to the basement. She stepped through the door once she felt confident no one was around.

She glanced at Rafe, then pointed to the stairs. They crept to the stairs and slowly ascended to the kitchen. The kitchen was clean. No dishes laying around, but there was a note on the counter. She padded toward the note.

"Miss Adelaide. I have made meals for you and Mr. Martin. They are in containers in the refrigerator. Heating instructions are on the lids. Catalina."

She left the note where it was, opened the refrigerator and saw the individual meal containers. There were many. Addy giggled. Catalina had been cooking up a storm.

She glanced at Rafe, who nodded in appreciation, then closed the door and moved toward the office. Nothing seemed out of place. She turned to ascend the grand staircase to the bedrooms above. Hers was at the top and to the right. Entering the bedroom, she saw nothing out of the ordinary. She stepped to the closet and pulled her travel bag from inside and swiftly tossed her clothing into it. No time to be neat. A movement outside caught her attention. She turned to Rafe and pointed to the window. They both neared the window cautiously. A black SUV slowly crawled down the street. As it neared the Bowman home, it slowed. Addy hurried from the room and to the room at the end of the hall, with windows to the front of the house. She crept to the side of the window and peered around the edge. The SUV had stopped, but no one had gotten out. Rafe stepped behind her, peering over her head. He whispered, "Is that one of yours?"

She shook her head.

Rafe pulled his phone from his pocket and texted someone.

Addy stepped away from the wall, "Stay here and watch them. I'm getting my weapons."

She hurried to her bedroom, pulled her weapon from its holster on her waist and checked the magazine. Satisfied it was full, she pulled a second weapon from her travel bag, inserted a full magazine and set it on the bed. She pulled a third from her travel bag and repeated. Tucking one of the extra weapons in her ankle holster and strapping it on, she then grabbed the third and moved back to the bedroom where Rafe stood watching.

Entering the room, she approached Rafe. He whispered, "Passenger door is opening. It's also not one of mine."

She looked around him, saw someone clad in all black slowly approaching the house. She handed Rafe the weapon. Two police cruisers pulled up behind the black SUV.

Rafe whispered, "They're going to arrest me."

"Let's get out of here." She moved toward the staircase, it would do them no good to be stuck up here in case they stormed the house. She slipped quietly down the staircase. As she reached the bottom of the stairs, the doorbell rang. She froze for a moment, and waited to see what would happen next.

The doorbell rang again and she moved around the staircase, toward the kitchen. Pounding sounded on the front door and the handle began to jiggle as if he was trying to get inside.

They hurried down the stairs to the basement and out the tunnel, locking the door behind them. Addy ran down the tunnel toward the opening, Rafe close behind her. She climbed the metal rungs, entered the code in the keypad and twisted the handle to open the hatch. She climbed out and waited for Rafe before closing it up and moving the rubber mat into place. Rafe jumped into the SUV and waited for her.

33

"Get out of the state."

"Roger."

Addie turned his phone, which he kept here in her hand. "I just texted Tate and told him we are on our way to the airport."

Rafe tapped the garage door button and as soon as he had enough room, he eased from the garage. Closed the door and sped down the street before they came around. He drove faster than he was comfortable given the streets were narrow, but didn't want to take the chance he'd be caught, so he pushed forward. As he turned out of the neighborhood, he sped a bit more, first exiting the surrounding neighborhood, then moving toward the highway.

Addy called Tate. "We're on the highway."

"Okay. I have a lead on where the body is, I'm sending someone to check it out. If it's where I think it is, we'll steal it back. They won't have it for evidence to use against Rafe."

"Thanks."

"Watch your backs. Gavin is waiting for you."

Rafe's stomach knotted. This is the sort of thing his father would be involved in. Not murder, but running and hiding. He'd spent his life avoiding trouble such as this. But now, here he was smack in the middle of it.

"Which way?" He barked out.

Addy gave him clear directions, then softly said, "You didn't do anything wrong. You're not in trouble, so to speak."

"They could put me in jail for a long time for something I didn't do. If King wants to destroy my credibility so no one believes me, he'll do it. Unless I give up Wade, which I won't."

"Hopefully Wade will get to the people he needs to get to first."

Rafe's jaw tightened as he ground his teeth together. He'd worked his entire life for his credibility. It rankled him to no end they'd try to destroy him. He was merely the second-hand recipient of damaging information on someone who shouldn't have any credibility. But the media had been quashed and evidence buried. People were coerced into silence for fear of shit just like this happening to them.

Rafe turned into the airport property and moved steadily toward the private hangars.

"It's hangar G7."

He found row G and turned left. The numbers were

visible on the doors of each hangar. As he passed Hangar 6, the door to 7 began to open.

"Park inside."

Turning the SUV into the hangar, he parked along the left side of the hangar where there was plenty of room for the SUV. Addy jumped from the vehicle and pulled her laptop from the backseat. He did the same. They jogged to the plane, whose steps had been lowered and a man stood outside waiting for them.

Addy spoke first. "Hi, Gavin. Thanks for coming for us. As usual, we're in a bit of a pickle."

"I understand Ms. Masters."

The man nodded to him as he began ascending the stairs. "Hello, Mr. Martin. I'm Gavin."

"Hello, Gavin. Thank you for your expedience."

He merely grinned then turned to the plane and waited until they were both inside before raising the steps from the plane. The thunking and noises coming from the plane were welcome right now. It meant they were on their way.

Addy sat in a seat in the middle of the plane. Two seats together with a table in front of them, two facing seats on the opposite side of the table.

"You're all set up here." He noted.

"We are. We won't have internet until we're up in the air, but we can work while we travel."

Light filled the hangar as the doors slid open and the lights dimmed in the cabin of the plane. Rafe sat across from Addy and watched her buckle her seat belt, then she laid her head back and stared at him.

He buckled his seatbelt and mimicked her, happy to gaze into her eyes. The plane began moving forward and his heartbeat raced. How far behind them were the police?

Turning his head, he watched out the window as Gavin taxied them past the hangars in row G. His breathing became stilted as the anticipation of being stopped tightened his body and made it difficult to breathe.

Gavin turned them left and proceeded to a smaller runway used by the private plane owners.

Turning right, he lined them up on the runway and they waited for a few beats.

Gavin's voice came over a speaker. "We've been given the all clear to take off. Please fasten your seatbelts."

His eyes sought Addy's. Her full lips turned up into a smile. "Gavin has flown GHOST out of some of the worst places. He's Navy trained and he's good. We've been under fire more times than I care to count. He's got this."

Rafe grinned. "I guess I shouldn't play poker with you."

Her giggle was adorable, welcomed, and enticing. "I guess I want to play poker with you now."

He chuckled and glanced out the window as the plane began moving down the runway. Their speed increased, the thumping of the uneven pavement beneath them welcome. Soon, they were in the air and a few minutes later, the landing gear hydraulics hummed as the wheels tucked into the belly of the plane.

Gavin spoke over the intercom once again. "We're safely up. We'll be flying at ten thousand feet and in the air for about two hours. Sit back and enjoy the flight folks."

Addy leaned forward, twisted the table between them so the oval filled the two seats on either side of them. She slowly moved across the narrow space between them and perched herself on his lap, her legs on either side of his. Her hands pushed into his hair and held his head, her lips, so soft and enticing, melded with his.

His hands found her backside and squeezed tightly while pulling her body into his firmly. He'd never joined the mile high club, but if he was joining today, there's no one he'd rather be with. She'd been teasing his thoughts for a few days now.

Her lips left his and his disappointment was short-lived as they planted soft kisses across his forehead and down the side of his face. When she reached his jaw, she nipped it a few times, her husky voice whispering. "When you're tense, I see your jaw clench and grind."

She planted a few more kisses on his jaw, then moved to the other side and repeated her kissing pattern. After nibbling on his right jaw, she moved her kisses down his neck. His hands squeezed her ass once again and pulled her into the hardness she'd created. She giggled slightly and lifted her head. When her eyes landed on his, they were dark, and sexy, and incredibly mesmerizing.

He swallowed to moisten his throat. "You want to join the mile high club Addy?" He didn't recognize his voice just then. Deep and gravely.

Her lips curved into a soft beguiling smile. When she spoke, it was soft and sexy. "I absolutely do."

He stared at her. "Me too." She bent down and kissed his lips. This time it wasn't the soft melding of lips but excitement and urgency.

His hands dug under her shirt and felt her heated skin. Her body was muscular and firm, but her breasts were full and soft. It was a beautiful contrast. He pinched her nipples and heard her gasp. She pulled away from him, just enough to look into his eyes.

Slowly she moved back, her legs moved from the seat until she was standing before him. She moved her hands to unzip her tactical slacks. Slowly. Their eyes never wavered. Shimmying her slacks over her slender hips, she let them drop to the floor, then moved her panties down her hips and legs. She stepped free from them, then slid her hands around the hem of her t-shirt and lifted it over her head. The soft blue lacy bra she wore contrasted with her olive skin. Her hands reached behind her back and unsnapped her bra easily, then she let the soft material slide down her arms and pile on the floor with the rest of her clothing.

Rafe stared at her gorgeous body. All of it. She was a goddess. He unzipped his pants and lifted his hips up as he pushed them down his hips and let them fall to his ankles. He reached down and stepped out of them, pulling a condom from his wallet quickly, then did the same with his boxer briefs. The cool air on his hot penis further hardened him. Addy's eyes dropped to his cock and it pulsed of its own accord. He pulled his t-shirt over his head and dropped it on the ever-growing pile on the floor.

Addy stepped forward and resumed her position over him. He dug his fingers into the soft flesh of her ass and pulled her forward until her body touched his hardened cock. She moved her hips back and forth and he huffed out a long breath.

"You feel incredible," he whispered.

She moved her sexy hips again as her lips pressed near his ear. "So do you."

She reached back and took the condom from his hand, ripped it open and pumped his cock a few times, watching the precum form before swiping it over the head. His breathing ratcheted up as her hands manipulated him in the sexiest way. He'd never felt like this before, he was sure of it.

She put the condom on the head of his cock, and slowly rolled it over him. Her hands doing a myriad of things to his body, his mind, his existence.

Once she'd finished, she rose up slightly, held his cock in her hand and perched herself over him, tucking the tip of his cock at her entrance. It was only by sheer control he didn't come right then. Her tight nipples were even with his mouth, so he leaned forward and sucked her left breast into his mouth and his hands gripped her hips and pushed her slowly down his cock.

She moaned softly as he filled her and he sucked harder before lifting her and plunging her down again. Her hands dug into his shoulders as she rose and fell over and over.

His skin heated, his mind nearly went blank as her body pleasured his. He pushed himself lower onto the seat, so she landed fully onto his cock and they both moaned. She increased the pace. He wouldn't make it long like this. Her full beautiful breasts bounced in front of his face which made him harder if that was even possible.

Addy kept the pace fast and furious. He didn't want it to end. "You feel incredible, Addy."

She smiled, her skin held a fine sheen which made her sexier. "So do you," she huffed out.

He tightened his hold on her hips, helping her movements so she didn't tire. He wanted her as long as she wanted him. Probably longer.

She dropped down on him and moaned. She tucked her face in the crook of his shoulder and neck, another moan rushed out and her body shuddered. He gave her a moment. He wanted to remember this forever. This moment right here. How she felt and sounded.

Addy took a deep breath, then pulled back. A sexy smile formed on her luscious lips. "Your turn."

She began riding him again, up and down, continuing the pace she'd set before. It didn't take long though. He stiffened as his balls drew up inside, the pain of them drawing up tightly was followed by the pleasure of his climax as he spilled himself inside of her. He groaned. At least he thought he did. His hearing seemed temporarily gone. He could only see spots before his eyes, but he felt Addy's naked warm body pressed into his chest, her hands digging into his hair, and that was heavenly.

...him now, and ... made from the bathroom ... side of the plane. He bent down, kissed her lips, then sat across from her with a devilish smile on his face.

"What are you grinning at?"

"You."

"Why is that?" She smiled at him because she couldn't believe... and became putty in his hands.

"I just made you mine. I like that."

"You made me yours? What on earth have you been smoking?"

His brows furrowed. "I'm not smoking anything sweetheart. I believe you came over here and initiated sex. Which means, you wanted it as bad as I did. And now, you're all mine."

She laughed. It felt good to laugh. It had been an incredibly long time. "That means I made you mine. Not the other way around."

He chuckled. He was incredible. Handsome. Smart. Oh, and he felt so flipping good.

Her phone rang and she answered without looking at the number or name on the phone.

"Adelaide Masters."

"Addy, it's Tate. Put me on speaker please."

She looked at her phone, tapped the speaker icon, twisted the table into place and laid her phone on the table.

"Go ahead Tate, Rafe can hear now."

Rafe sat up straighter, playtime was over. Life came crashing down.

Tate began. "Okay. We have the body. I sent Hawk and Josh to retrieve it. Hawk has a contact at a funeral home there who has it on ice now. It was at the morgue near Camp David. King somehow has access to that already. He's moving fast. I think he knows this information is out there and he needs to wrap things up quickly so he can be confirmed and sworn in. The senator gave us that little tidbit. He's scared and knows his life is short if he's found. We have him in a safehouse here. When you land, come straight to the HOG. You'll stay here where we have security and can monitor things."

"Okay. What about Brett Selisen? He's the one that entered Rafe's house and planted the blood. He's also the person who likely stole the body in the first place."

"He is. We have footage from the morgue entrance. He and another man entered the morgue while our coroner was doing paperwork with a family member of a decedent." Tate's chair squeaked. "But, Selisen is likely a bit player. He's doing the dirty work for King. Just like Senator Jackson did before. My best guess is King will turn on Selisen as soon as the heat is turned up on him. I just spoke to Casper, he has a man on the inside at the White House and who is having regular meetings with Vice President-Elect Chad Marshall. He's been briefed and is currently hiding out in a safe house while this can be sorted. He doesn't want to be brought into the murder of the Chief of Staff of Yerezdan, Bertrum Malachi, in any way, shape, or form. He wasn't involved in it and he doesn't want anything to bleed over to destroy his reputation. King isn't aware Marshall is any the wiser."

Rafe sat forward. "Tate, how is this going to play out?"

Tate blew out a breath. "We have to put things in order. Actually, Casper is working on that. The documents are uploaded to our system and Casper has access. He's making contact with people he trusts to bring King down. The murder has been confirmed and with the senator's help, we have the names of the men who committed the murder. They won't be picked up until everything is ready to push out. It'll only alert King that something going on. And we need to make sure Chad Marshall is on board and ready to take over if this works."

Rafe sat back. Addy grinned at him, then spoke to Tate. "Tate, Brett Selisen is a traitor. We know he had some big medical bills and turned against Rafe and spied on him for payment. I'd like him brought down right away. He also planted evidence and stole a body. Can you plant evidence in Selisen's bank records to make it look like he's hacked into the bank and stolen money? That would get him picked up on other charges and put him out of commission for trying to discredit Rafe."

Tate chuckled. "I think we can handle that. Piper from RAPTOR is great at doing that."

"That gives Rafe a little payback to Selisen and keeps Selisen's mind on his own shit not Rafe."

"Okay. On it. Anything else?"

She stared at Rafe, raised her brows and waited. Rafe's chest rose and fell. "Nothing at this time."

"Okay. I'll see you in a while."

The line went dead and she watched Rafe. He didn't seem happy or excited that his reputation would remain intact.

"What's wrong?"

"I don't like planting evidence to get Selisen in trouble. That's the sort of bullshit my father would do."

"It's temporary. It'll be removed once we have King and can turn over all the other criminal activities Selisen has partaken in."

Rafe shrugged. "Still doesn't feel right."

She pushed the table aside again and moved to sit on his lap. Her legs hung over the armrest, and into the seat next to him.

"Right now, we have burner phones on the plane. You should use one to call Leesha and tell her you had to get out of town. Tell her you're in Hawaii. If her phone is bugged, they'll hear that and look for you there."

His voice was a low growl when he responded. "What would I be doing in Hawaii?"

"Senator Jackson said his family had a place in Hawaii. So, you're doing some investigation. Highly top secret. A matter of national security. Anything that will make King think he's sent you on a wild goose chase. But he'll also worry that Jackson hid documents there. He'll likely send someone to check and keep his focus there for a while."

"Does GHOST have the senator's family?"

"Yes. They are in a safe house. It's undisclosed to us right now."

"What will telling Leesha I'm in Hawaii do for me?"

"It'll throw him off the scent. Selisen saw Myles, Henry, and I with the senator in the bar. I'm sure he's been investigating us. We're, for the most part, off the grid when it comes to social media and such. But, if he has access to military records, we're there. So are our parents. Casper, Gaige, and Tate have tried securing our records so they aren't easily accessed. But the President of the United States, or newly-elected president, may have people who will do some shady shit to uncover what we've hidden."

... minutes.
... She ... her head ... Her scent filled his ... filled up every empty well he had in his life.

"What's the HOG?"

She giggled. "It's where we live. Home. Office. Garage. HOG. It's an old factory we converted."

He ... He nodded. "Okay. Let me think about it."

His stomach tightened. This was shady shit like his dad had done over the years. Was this for the greater good? Maybe. He needed to do it to keep her safe though. It would be his fault if King latched on to Addy or her teammates because he didn't do everything he could to keep her safe. He'd do shady shit for her. He absolutely would.

Addy kissed his lips, then moved to get the phone. Her loss was immediate. He liked having her close. He liked being with her. He absolutely wanted to have sex with her. Again and again.

She reappeared with a phone in a package and opened it up. He watched her fingers tap on the phone, start it up, set a password. All the things. She'd done this a few times in her life.

"How long have you been an operative?" He questioned.

Her lips turned up on one side. It was adorable. "You've read my file. I assume you know that."

"I want you to tell me."

She stopped messing with the phone and stared at him. "About eight years now. I left the military when I was twenty-four. It was a given I'd work for GHOST. All of us knew we'd work for GHOST. So, at the ripe old age of twenty-four, I became a GHOST."

"How many missions have you been on?"

She sat back, a smile on her face. "So you want to get to know me better? Is that what this is? Or are you stalling?"

He leaned back and took a deep breath. "Maybe both."

She nodded once. "I've been on countless missions. Some stick out, some don't. Gaige and Tate have all the specifics. What I do know is they take care of us. We'd just come off a particularly bad mission when we were sent to Kentucky. Kentucky was low-key. It was a money maker for GHOST. It kept us employed and yet, it wasn't hard. That's the longest mission I've ever been on."

"What was the most dangerous?"

She leaned forward and laid her arms on the table between them. "We were sent to a rain forest in Nicaragua to rescue two American soldiers who were kidnapped. It was dirty. It was dangerous. The guerrillas there don't like outsiders and they shoot first. They were holding our soldiers in shitty pits in the ground. They weren't feeding them well, but they were guarding the shit out of them. We had to go in undetected and kill off the guerrillas one at a time, quietly, until our men were not guarded. Pull them out of the pit and get them to safety."

His eyes never left hers. His jaw twitched and he realized he was grinding his teeth.

"I don't like that for you."

She chuckled. "I do. It's what I was born to do. For as long as I can, I will do it. Gaige and Tate do a good job of training us. They also know when to let us rest. I get to do work I love and that has significant meaning. I make great money doing it. And, I'm working with family and friends I love and who love me. That is something most people never get to do."

He nodded once. "That's very true." He heaved out a breath. "It's also dangerous."

Her phone rang and she slowly lifted it up. Her brows furrowed as she looked at her screen. "Adelaide Masters."

Her brows furrowed more, then she pulled her phone away from her ear and tapped the speaker icon. As she set it on the table, she said, "Can you repeat that please? You cut out on me."

"I said, I know who you are. I know you saw me at the bar and watched me follow the senator out of the bar. I also believe you stole something that belongs to me."

"I didn't steal anything. I believe you stole something that belongs to me. I just took it back."

"You and Rafe think you're so fucking smart, don't you? Well, let me tell you this. I'll find you. I won't stop until I do. And, I'll find Rafe. I'll make both of you tell me where Senator Jackson and Wade Evans are. You're harboring them. But I'll find them."

"Well, have you thought maybe you could work for us? Maybe we can protect you from Senator King."

"President King."

"Not yet."

"He will be soon enough. I have his protection."

"You mean like he protected Senator Jackson? He turned on him as soon as he wasn't useful anymore. What makes you think he won't do the same thing to you?"

"Consider yourself warned. I'll find you. I'll make you pay. You and your teammates and Rafe Martin."

The line went silent and she tapped her phone a couple of times. Ringing came over the speaker.

"Vickers."

"It's Addy. Did you get that phone call?"

"Yes. We're tracing it."

"Thank you. I'm asking Rafe to call his office and tell his assistant he's in Hawaii on a case of national security."

"Great idea. Piper is working on Selisen's bank records now. We should be able to have him picked up by the authorities in about an hour. Bank fraud is a serious offense."

"Wonderful. We'll be landing in about a half hour."

"See you then."

His stomach tightened. His mouth was dry and his body felt as cold as a frozen lake. "Addy. Give me that phone."

She finished setting it up and handed it to him. He tapped out his office number and listened to the ringing. He tapped the speaker button and held the phone between them.

"Office of Special Counselor Rafe Martin. How may I help you?"

"Leesha, it's Rafe."

"Mr. Martin. I've been so worried. Brett has been trying to touch base with you and I've been worried something happened to you. Brett said your home was broken into. Are you alright?"

Here it was, his first lie. "I'm fine Leesha. I had to leave the state to research something for Wade Evans. I'm in Hawaii and will be for a few days at a minimum. I'm sorry to have worried you, but this trip was unplanned, and it came up quickly."

Leesha huffed out a deep breath. "Oh. Whew. Thank you for contacting me. I'll direct questions and inquiries accordingly. Should I clear your calendar?"

"Yes, please clear my calendar for the rest of this week and next week. I'll take it day by day here and let you know how my investigation is going and when I'll return."

"Thank you, Mr. Martin. I'll take care of it."

"Thank you, Leesha. I'll check in periodically."

He ended their call and sat back. He felt disgusting having to lie to someone who trusted him and had given him her all. It was a feeling he didn't want to repeat again.

36

She buckled her seat belt, then watched Rafe woodenly fasten his. She smiled at his handsome face when his eyes met hers. Then she saw his jaw twitch.

"You can apologize to Leesha when this is sorted and you're safe. If she cares for you, she'll understand."

He could have been considering this. She leaned forward and laid her hand on the table, palm up. His jaw twitched again, but slowly his hand locked with hers. She squeezed and held his hand tightly. "It's necessary, Rafe."

"I know."

The plane touched down. As was Gavin's way, it was smooth as silk. She grinned and squeezed Rafe's hand once again.

Rafe grinned. "He's good."

Nodding, she chuckled. "That he is."

Gavin taxied to their hangar and as soon as he'd

stopped, they both unbuckled their seatbelts, gathered their laptop cases and waited to exit the plane. Gavin stood at the door.

She smiled and nodded. "Thank you, Gavin. A perfect flight as always."

"Thank you, Ms. Masters."

Rafe held his hand out to Gavin. "Thank you for your expedience, Gavin."

"You're welcome, Mr. Martin."

As she descended the stairs, a black Jeep pulled to a stop near the hangar. She giggled and ran to the Jeep.

Maya jumped from the Jeep and wrapped her in a hug. It felt good to see her again. It had only been a week, but that seemed too long.

Maya pulled back and looked into her face. "How are you?"

"I'm good. I do have someone I'd like you to meet though."

She turned and held her hand out to Rafe. He had made his way toward them, at a slower pace than she had. He took her hand in his and squeezed.

"Rafe, this is my cousin, Maya. Maya and Myles are brother and sister. Twins, actually."

Rafe nodded and grinned. "It's nice to meet you, Maya."

Maya's eyes darted between them for a few beats. Then her lips turned up into a devilish smile. "I think there are a few things I need to know. For instance, what's happening here?" She motioned between Rafe and her. Addy's smile grew so big it almost hurt. Just as she was about to respond, Rafe's voice came out husky and sexy. "We're together."

"Well, now, look at that." Maya responded.

Addy's cheeks burned hot. They shouldn't, but she was the first in their family, of this generation, to bring home someone special. And, that's what this felt like. Bringing home someone special. She suddenly felt a pang of sadness that her parents weren't here today to meet Rafe. She'd absolutely love to introduce them to Rafe. Maybe they'd come up for a visit soon.

Maya sized them up. Standing before her as if they were waiting for approval, hand in hand. Maya smiled her big bright sassy smile and nodded. "You two look good together."

Addy let out a short breath. She'd actually held it for a moment. Sometimes, Maya was unpredictable. Not in a bad way, but in a way that she'd say exactly what was on her mind. She was just like Aunt Jax in that way. Myles was more like Uncle Dodge in that he didn't say much. But when he did say something, it had merit.

Addy turned to see Rafe grinning. "It's because of Addy. She makes me look good."

Maya laughed. It was an out loud laugh. "Right. So, come on. Tate's waiting for you two."

Addy and Rafe followed Maya to her Jeep. It was a four door, so easy to get into. She picked the backseat because she didn't want Rafe to have to sit in the back.

"Addy, I can sit back there if you want to chat with Maya." His husky voice floated over her. It did things to her. She shook her head, as much to clear her thoughts from what his voice did to her as to tell him no. "I'm good, Rafe. Sit up front. Maya and I can chat while I'm in the back seat too. And, honestly, it's only been a week since we've seen each other."

He watched her climb in, then set her laptop case on the floor in front of her legs. Before he closed the door, he winked at her and that did more than his voice did. She smiled at him and he closed his eyes. Hopefully that was a good thing.

Rafe climbed in the seat in front of her. Maya in the driver's seat. She easily maneuvered them from the lot where the hangars were and to the road that led them into Glen Hollow and the HOG.

"What's been going on here, Maya?"

Maya shrugged and looked at her in the mirror. "Myles and Spencer are guarding the senator. Henry went home to help Everleigh with the horses. They're having another baby soon."

"Really, who?"

"Queen. Can you believe that?"

"Wow. That's awesome."

She saw Rafe turn as Maya chatted and she giggled. "Rafe, Queenie is one of the horses. Henry and Everleigh have rescued abused horses and they've now set out to breed them and sell the foals. Some of the horses they rescued actually have great pedigrees. That was a bonus."

"That's admirable. I'd like to go see them. I haven't been around horses in years."

Maya nodded. "First Tate. I promised. But once you're settled in, we can go out and see them. I love visiting their farm."

Addy asked, "Have they set a wedding date yet?"

Maya shook her head. "Not that I've heard. But that doesn't mean they haven't. I was called out on a short mission to help rescue a woman kidnapped by her ex-husband."

"How short?"

"In and out. Literally, only one over-night."

"Sweet."

Maya pulled into the driveway at the HOG, waved her key card to open the gate and drove to the back of the building where their garage doors were located.

She pulled into her spot in the garage and Addy unbuckled her seat belt and started opening the door when it opened on its own.

Rafe stood with his hand out to her and a sexy grin on his face. "It's time you let me use my manners."

She took his hand, a smile on her face that bunched her cheeks. It felt good to smile so often. She was generally a happy person, but she'd never had someone special make her smile so often. "Thank you."

He bent down and kissed her lips. He went to the back of the Jeep and opened the tailgate, pulled his bag from the back then took her hand as they entered the HOG. Maya had already gone inside.

As they neared the door, Rafe looked around the garage with its posters and decorations and whistled. "This is beautiful."

"Sophie, Tate's mom and Bridget, Aidyn's mom did most of the decorating. When we go out to Henry's, my mom and Henry's mom, Roxanne did most of their house. We're fortunate to have such talented women in our families. We'll all have nice homes one day. If we choose."

"What is your alternative?"

She shrugged. "Living here. Tate and Lara do. Spencer and Kenna do too. The entire second floor has been remodeled recently to allow for larger living quarters. Tate and Lara have Barrett, who's six months old now. And Spencer and Kenna will likely have kids one day, so they have three-bedroom suites upstairs. There's room for a couple more up there too."

"Is that what you want to do?"

She stopped walking and turned to him. "I honestly don't know. It will depend on who I marry and what he wants."

[illegible] anyone but [illegible] they'd only known [illegible] a short time. Though, he felt like he'd known her for a long time. He'd read her files. All of their files. He'd gotten to know her through her body of work. And her family members' work. He'd known of her for years. Getting to know her these past few days was exciting.

He [illegible] into the HOC and the kitchen smelled amazing. It was seven o'clock in the evening and it smelled like it was dinnertime.

A woman in her late fifties or so stood at the stove, stirring something that smelled fantastic. Fruity and fattening.

Addy grinned. "Hi, Helissa. Rafe, this is Helissa our cook and housekeeper. Helissa, this is Rafe."

Helissa wiped her hands on an apron around her waist. He immediately thought of Catalina. He held his hand out to her, and when she gripped his hand in a firm handshake, he knew she was no-nonsense and trustworthy. She looked him in the eye. "It's nice to meet you, Rafe."

"Addy, it's nice to have you home. I have your room ready and I have Henry's old room ready for Rafe."

Helissa looked at Rafe and smiled.

Rafe put his arm around Addy. "I'll be staying with Addy. But I do appreciate your hard work in putting together a room for me."

Helissa's cheeks turned bright pink. "I'm so sorry. I wasn't aware..."

Addy touched Helissa's arm. "Please don't worry. No one knew until now. We're...new."

Maya entered the kitchen and leaned against the counter watching them chat. She had a sassy grin on her face, that was for certain.

Addy turned toward the living area. "Rafe, I'll show you where our room is."

As they passed Maya, she said, "Do Uncle Josh, and Auntie Isabella know?"

Addy stopped and her cheeks flamed hot. He stared at Maya and grinned. "We haven't told them yet. But, we will soon."

Maya smiled and stepped to the refrigerator and pulled out a bottle of water. Addy pulled him to the bedroom. As they entered the room, he lowered his voice. "She won't tell your parents before you do, will she?"

Addy giggled. "No. She's just trying to get a rise out of us and embarrass me. It's all good. One day she'll meet someone, and I'll do the same to her."

"I can't believe she hasn't met someone yet. She's quite stunning." He pulled her into his arms. "Not as stunning as you are, but I can see the family resemblance."

He kissed her lips and her arms came around his

waist. Tipping his head slightly, he fit his lips over hers better, and allowed himself to sink deeper into her. His life had been turned upside down since he'd met her and to save his soul, he was surprised as hell that he wasn't more bothered by it all. He was in the thick of something major, yet he just knew it would work out for the best.

He reluctantly pulled away and rested his forehead against hers. "Adelaide Masters, I am so enamored by you. You have captivated my entire being."

He could feel her heartbeat against his chest. Her breathing became uneven. "You've done the same to me, Rafe. It's scary how much you consume my thoughts."

They pulled away. Reluctantly. He looked around the room. It was a palate of neutrals, grays, and browns. Antique bedside tables framed the bed. A headboard of gray material took up a good portion of the wall above the bed. A matching gray fabric sofa with tan pillows sat directly across from the bed. It fit together wonderfully. A television hung from the wall across from both the bed and the sofa.

"I have a bathroom here to the left. If you want to put your things in there, I'll make some room after we speak with Tate."

"Thank you." He set his bag on the floor near the sofa and held his hand out to her. "Let's go see Tate."

They moved in unison out of the bedroom and toward a door across the massive living area. Three large brown leather sofas with white fluffy blankets sat in a U-shape in the middle of this room. A television hung from the exposed brick wall across from the sofas. A large glass cubicle with an old oak table sat just outside and to the right of Addy's room. "That's our conference room."

They stopped behind the sofa facing the television

and she pointed out the rooms. "Maya's room is behind the conference room and in the corner over there. The two bedrooms across from the conference room against the back wall are empty. We use them for guests. Our parents visit a lot. That door is the front door. It faces the road but it's almost never used. The room on the left of the front door, is Henry's old room. Next to that, is Spencer's old room. He and Kenna live upstairs now. Myles' bedroom is in that corner. Leading around the room and to the left is Tate's old bedroom, now empty, and then the office. Next to the office is a storage room. On the other side of the storage room and accessed from the garage is our shooting range."

"Holy shit. You have a shooting range here? That's fantastic."

"We're pretty self-contained here. We have a workout facility in the garage too. I'll show you that later."

She took his hand again and led him across the floor to Tate's office. The door was partially open, but she knocked twice then pushed the door open.

Tate sat behind his desk on a laptop, typing away. "Hey there, Addy and Rafe. Come in, please."

Tate closed the lid on his laptop. He stood and held his hand out. Rafe quickly clasped hands with Tate and shook vigorously. "It's great to meet you in person Tate. Thank you for the plane ride here."

Tate nodded. His eyes glanced at Addy briefly before he nodded. "Welcome home, Addy."

"Thanks."

Tate sat and motioned to two chairs in front of his desk. "Okay. Let's start with new news. I was just informed from a friendly police officer in D.C., that Selisen was picked up on bank fraud. Our friendly remembered his name as the person associated with your office, Rafe, and contacted me. I asked him to indeed pick him up. He's in a holding cell for tonight. He'll get his time before a judge tomorrow and bail may be set. I'm working with the prosecutor there to demand that he not be allowed bail. Since he's committed bank fraud, it'll take some time to ascertain which of his funds were fraudulently obtained and shouldn't be used as bail."

The mention of Selisen soured his stomach. It had since he'd learned of Selisen's betrayal. He was grateful Selisen was in jail and no longer allowed in the office. Tomorrow, he'd call Leesha and explain to her that Selisen was no longer allowed in his office, and he'd send word that Selisen was no longer employed either.

"Thank you, Tate. I appreciate all you're doing for me."

Tate grinned. "We're doing all of it for the good of the country. You shouldn't have been dragged into it. But, as soon as the senator visited Wade, you were brought in by proxy."

He nodded. Turning his head to look at Addy, he grinned. "I think I gained something much more valuable in the end."

Addy smiled at him and reached over and took his hand in hers. He winked at her and her cheeks turned an adorable shade of pink.

Turning back to Tate, he saw Tate's brows lift. Tate nodded. "I had no idea you two had grown so close. But, you're right. She's very valuable."

Tate turned to Addy. "You better call your mom and dad."

She chuckled. "I will."

Rafe's phone rang. He saw Wade's name. "It's Wade. I need to take this."

Tate nodded and Rafe stood to leave. "Hi, Wade. I'm here with Tate and Addy."

"You can put me on speaker phone then."

Rafe turned and set his phone on Tate's desk. Tapping the speaker icon, he said, "Okay. You're on speaker."

"President-elect King has announced the appointment of three cabinet members. All of these men have ties in Yerezdan. They'll likely work hard to keep the dirty deeds of Yerezdan under wraps. Also, it's believed the oil for arms deals will continue with this president. Many people will perish due to these deals. We're running out of time to get this information out. We're down to four weeks."

Rafe leaned forward. "What do you need us to do?"

"I'm not sure right now. I'll text you all some names I need researched. I think these will be people we can approach to help us. All on other sides of the aisle, of course. Rafe, you'll need to be on the secret server when you research them. Security at the White House will be pinged if we search them outside of that. Also, Rafe, research the Constitution and any subsequent executive orders surrounding ethics and conduct of elected members when conducting illegal activities."

"Okay. Send me the names you want researched, and in the meantime, I'll begin researching the rest."

Wade continued. "Tate, we may need more help from RAPTOR cyber unit."

Tate nodded. "They'll help us without complaint."

Wade cleared his throat. "Addy. I understand Selisen called and threatened you. He's likely blustering on in jail and spilling his information or threatening to. Stay alert. If he has your name and phone number, he'll likely be able to figure out where you're located."

"Thank you. We'll remain vigilante."

"I'm working on my end to resecure your records. Thank you all. I'll be in touch."

The line went silent and Rafe stood. "I'll need somewhere to work, please."

Tate nodded. "Set up in the conference room. Addy, and anyone else available will help you in your research."

...for the ... them out on the ... their bedroom with his laptop case. He'd showered and changed clothes. He wore tan khakis and a black three button placket shirt which showed off his muscles.

His eyes landed on hers and held. His posture was straight and tall. In a word, he was delicious.

He came closer, leaned in, and the aroma of his shower soap and aftershave filled her senses. That fabulous odor combined with his physique, was impossible not to notice. It was impossible not to drool.

He stopped next to her, leaned in and kissed her. She liked it. Then she saw Maya entering the living area from the kitchen and she remembered she needed to call her parents.

"I have to call my mom."

Rafe cocked his head. "Okay. Gotta tell you, I'm not sure how it makes me feel that when I kiss you, you want to call your mom."

She giggled. "No, I just saw Maya." She pointed to her cousin nearing the conference room. "I better call Mom and Dad before Maya tells Auntie Jax or Uncle Dodge and they tell my parents about you."

He grinned. "Ah. Okay. I feel better."

She turned to leave but stopped. "What do I tell them? Are we...exclusive? Just sort of dating? Having sex on planes?"

He chuckled and kissed her again. Maya entered the glass room and scoffed. "Don't tell me you'll be doing a lot of that."

Rafe grinned, "I sure hope so."

He took her hand and pulled her from the confines of the glass walls. Leading them to their bedroom, he stepped inside, turned to face her and lowered his voice. "As far as I'm concerned, we're exclusive and together. I am completely enamored with you. I want to explore all we can explore with each other because I've never felt like this about another human in my life."

She stared into his eyes for a few moments. Her lips drew up into a smile. "Thank you. I feel the same way."

He kissed her again. "I've got to get to work. Call your parents."

She watched his sexy, tight ass walk away. Yeah, he was delicious.

She sat on the sofa, put her feet on the coffee table and dialed her mom's phone number. It rang only once, "Addy. Are you alright?"

She giggled. "I'm fine, Mamá. Better than fine."

"Your dad said you were in a situation. I hate that for you. Are you still in the situation?"

"I'm at the HOG. We're fine. My records were breached. Casper is working to resecure them."

Her mom let out a deep breath. "Thank god." She cleared her throat daintily. "I always worry when your father, you, Jax and Dodge, and Maya and Myles are out on missions and in situations."

"I know Mamá. I'm fine, I promise. But, I do have something to tell you."

"Oh, dear. Okay, I'm sitting."

She laughed. "It's not bad. Goodness, it's good. I met someone. I really, really like him. He's handsome and strong and smart and he cares for me."

"Oh, honey, that's just wonderful. I can't wait to meet him. What's his name and what does he do for a living?"

She giggled again, so happy to have this conversation with her mom. "His name is Rafe. I can't wait for you to meet him. He's here at the HOG with me. This mission has swallowed him up in it. But, we're working to take care of that and him. He's the Special Counsel for Wade at the Department of Defense."

"And, can he live with what you do? Sometimes, the lines are blurred. If he's an attorney, he may not be happy with that."

"That's a conversation we haven't had yet."

She heard her mom moving around the house, her breathing changed and she was quiet for a moment. She heard a muffled, "Josh, Addy met someone."

She heard the phone drop lightly on a surface, assuming it was her father's desk. "I have you on speaker and your dad is here Addy."

"Hi, Papá . I heard Mamá tell you about Rafe."

"Is this Rafe who works with Wade?"

"Yes." She grew nervous as she waited for her father to say something. She began picking at invisible lint on her slacks, then she twisted her hair around her finger. The bedroom door opened and Rafe entered the room. His grin sent butterflies to flight in her tummy. He sat on the sofa next to her and his scent, presence and heat were more than welcome.

"From everything I've heard about Rafe, he's a good man."

Rafe grinned at her. "Thank you, sir. I just entered the room."

"Rafe, as Addy's father, and the only man who has loved her to this point in her life, you need to know I take her life very seriously. Both Isi and I do. I understand things can happen between couples, but you better treat her right. You understand?"

Rafe stared at her, the grin on his face was impossible to look away from. "Yes, sir. I understand."

Her mom finally spoke. "I'm looking forward to meeting you in person, Rafe."

"I'm looking forward to meeting you as well Mrs. Masters."

"Isabella. Or Isi is what my friends call me."

"I'm looking forward to meeting you as well, Isi."

He leaned in and kissed her lips. "I'm sorry, but I have to get back to work. I simply wanted to meet you, even by phone."

Her parents spoke at the same time. "It was nice to meet you, Rafe."

He chucked her under the chin with his finger, winked at her and left the room. She had to work not to sigh.

Her mom interrupted her carnal thoughts. "Addy, when can we see you?"

"I hope soon Mamá. Let us get this mission sorted."

Commotion from the other room grabbed her attention. "Mamá, I have to go. I love you and Papa'."

"We love you too, Addy."

...dropping ...refrigerator for anything ...woman with long dark hair ...descended the staircase and slipped into Tate's office. Addy stepped into the living area and turned to the kitchen as Myles opened the refrigerator door.

"Helissa made you meals and put them on the middle shelf." She informed them.

Myles closed the refrigerator door and grinned. "Thanks."

Then his eyes peered above her head and straight into his. Addy turned and saw them staring at each other. She strode toward Myles.

"Rafe's here because King's men were trying to arrest him." She tucked her hands in her front pockets. "And he's with me."

Myles stopped staring at him and dropped his eyes to Addy. He pulled a meal container from the refrigerator and set it on the counter.

Spencer moved passed both of them and headed for the stairs.

Rafe stood and strode toward the kitchen. Myles watched him the entire time and Rafe inhaled a deep breath, ready for whatever was about to happen. He stopped next to Addy, put his arm around her shoulders and kissed the top of her head.

"Myles, Addy and I are together. I'm a good person. I won't hurt her."

Myles stared for a few moments, then his shoulders relaxed. "She doesn't have a brother, that falls to me." He looked at Addy. "I just want you safe and happy."

Addy stepped forward and reached across the counter to Myles' hand. He took her hand in his and she chuckled. "You're the best brother a girl could have. I am safe and I am happy."

Myles nodded. "Do Uncle Josh and Aunt Isi know?"

"Yes. I just got off the phone with them."

"Okay." He let go of Addy's hand and reached forward toward him. Rafe wrapped his hand around Myles' and shook.

Rafe asked, "Who's with the senator?"

"Henry and Tate are right now. Maya is going to relieve Tate at midnight."

"Rafe and I can relieve both of them. Henry will want to be home and so will Tate. Maya can rest tonight. We have research to do anyway, we can do it there."

Myles shrugged. "Great. Let Tate know." He picked up his food plate and popped it into the microwave. Addy turned to him. "You don't mind, do you?"

"Of course not."

Addy began texting Tate and he strode to the conference room and packed up his laptop and notepad.

He sauntered to the bedroom and pulled a jacket from his suitcase. Addy came in behind him.

"I made room for you in these drawers here." She opened three drawers on the right side of the dresser. He chuckled. "I don't have that many clothes here. One drawer will do."

She shrugged. "I also made room in the closet for you. There are extra hangars at the back."

He kissed her lips. Happy to do that whenever he wanted now and quickly stowed the clothing he had brought. He set his bag at the back of the closet and came out to find Addy pulling off her clothes. He cocked his head and stared at her.

She chuckled. "I'm jumping in the shower quick. We don't have to be there for an hour."

Sitting on the edge of the bed, he eagerly watched her strip down. Each layer more exciting than the last. "Are you going to watch me the entire time?"

"I'm thinking of joining you in the shower."

"But you just took a shower."

"Alone."

The smile that grew across her beautiful face was enticing. "Well, then. I wouldn't mind company."

She shimmied her panties off and walked her dirty clothes to a wicker hamper in the corner.

She passed him with a saucy look in her eyes, but too far away for him to grab her. She disappeared behind the shower door and his decision was made. Discarding his clothing in record time, he entered the bathroom. Steam rolled from the room when he opened the door and that was sexy.

Opening the shower door, he stepped in behind Addy, her long dark hair was wet and draped down her slender back. His cock rose to the occasion. He moved toward her until his cock nestled in the seam of her delicious ass. His hands slid over her naked body and held her full breasts in his hands.

Addy leaned forward, placing her hands on the wall of the shower, and he bent his knees, positioned his cock at her entrance, and slid inside. He closed his eyes as her warmth encased his cock like a glove. He moved in and out of her body, she pushed back into him with each thrust. Her breasts moved in his hands as he pumped into her. Her firm ass pushing against him as she swallowed his cock made him dizzy. He thrust into her over and over, his body heating, his mind filled with all things Addy.

She pulled his right hand from her breast down to her clit and he eagerly swirled over her sensitive tissue, ready for her to finish so he could.

He felt his climax coming. His balls began to draw up tightly. He pulled from her body and spun her around to face him. He hooked her left leg over his right arm and pushed into her once again. Her eyes closed briefly, then opened and stared into his. He fell into the depths of her dark eyes. Her sensual lips formed an "o" when he pushed into her. He pushed in and ground against her body, causing her to gasp and dig her fingers into his arms. He repeated that motion, over and over until she gasped and hung onto his arms tightly. He gave her a moment, a short one. Then he continued to pump into her until his balls were painfully tight and finally he came as spurt after spurt of cum filled her body.

He froze, concentrating on not falling, his knees were shaking and weak. She could bring him down in a heartbeat. Her hands slid over his back, slid down to his ass and squeezed him tightly, pulling him tightly to her even as he softened.

He closed his eyes once more, imprinting the feeling of being with her into his mind. He never wanted to forget how he felt when he was with her. Not just sexually, though that was amazing. But always. He looked for her in a room now. He felt whole when she was near. He always wanted to feel that.

[illegible] Blow [illegible] her head back in [illegible] were on duty tonight and needed to [illegible] the people Wade sent to them. Rafe had to study constitutional law and ethics charters. Exciting. But then again, she'd be with him the entire night, working and chatting when they took a break. The senator would likely be sleeping, so hopefully it would be peaceful.

[illegible] let it fall over her shoulders then exited the bathroom. Rafe sat on the sofa waiting for her. A sexy grin on his face when she entered the room.

"You look beautiful, Addy."

Her heartbeat increased just looking at him. "You look handsome, Rafe."

He winked then stood and moved toward her. He wrapped her in his arms and pulled her close. He kissed the top of her head then stepped back. "Ready?"

"Ready."

He pulled his laptop case off the bed, slipped the strap

over his head and waited for her. She picked up her laptop and slung it over her shoulder as she stepped to the door.

They padded out, ready for action and in work mode. Maya grinned as she stood and exited the conference room.

"Thanks for taking my shift tonight."

"You're welcome. Get some rest."

Maya chucked her on the shoulder, nodded at Rafe and went back to the conference room. Myles waved from the conference room, his empty plate next to him. She turned toward the kitchen and the door that led to the garage. After they'd closed the kitchen door behind them, Addy turned to Rafe. "Let me take a minute to show you the gun range and the workout room." Striding to the right she opened the outer door to the gun range. The lights clicked on to illuminate the outer room.

"This is where we stow our gear if we need to." Pointing to the left, "Eye protection, and ear protection are stored here." She opened locker doors to show him. Pointing to the right, "Flack vests are hanging in here." She opened another locker to show him the vests hanging.

She moved toward a door at the far end of the room and opened it. Lights flickered on. "This is the range. We only have three lanes, but that's enough for us."

"It's impressive."

"Aidyn's mom and dad built it for us. Bridget is a master marksman and owns her own gun range. She teaches classes and has a passion for self-defense."

"Wicked."

"Right." She turned and led the way out of the gun range to a door across the garage. "This is the workout room. It doesn't smell like gun powder, sadly, but usually sweat."

Rafe chuckled. "That's usually the case with any gym."

Pushing open the door, the lights clicked on and illuminated the room and all the equipment.

"Impressive. No expense has been spared."

She grinned. "That's the way Gaige works. He keeps us healthy, makes working out easy, gun range handy, and we get paid well. It works for all of us and we don't have turnover."

"That's the best part. I can only imagine how hard it is to find new operatives."

"Well, they were lucky with all of us. They birthed us. Not so sure that will happen again. But, I guess you never know."

Rafe nodded and exited the room. Addy turned and saw him staring at the vehicles.

"We'll take mine. The black Mustang."

He grinned. "Nice. That suits you."

She grinned. "You want to drive?"

His smile was genuine. "Absolutely."

She hopped into the passenger seat and Rafe adjusted the driver's seat, moving the seat all the way back.

He tapped the opener and started the Mustang, a grin on his face when it roared to life. Easing them from the garage, his smile grew. Addy added the address to the safe house into her phone and set it in the holder hanging from the rearview mirror.

As he drove through town, she told him about some businesses.

"There's Lara's bakery to the left, Lara's Delights. Wait till you have her cookies, they're fantastic. She's between Chestnut Grove furniture and Stackable Reads bookstore.

Tomorrow in the daylight, let's take a ride and I'll show you the town and Henry and Everleigh's place."

He chuckled. "That sounds fantastic."

They left the town behind and headed out to the country. Rafe turned down a county road, then onto a country road, and finally a gravel road. She grimaced slightly, her car would need to be washed tomorrow.

The house came into view, a small log cabin nestled at the base of the mountain. The scene was picturesque and peaceful. She texted Tate and announced their arrival. He gave her the thumbs-up.

"We're good to go in."

Rafe backed it up to the side of the cabin, alongside Henry's pickup. He turned to her, "Let me be a gentleman."

She giggled. "Okay."

He stepped from the Mustang and swiftly moved around to open her door. Holding his hand out for hers, a thrill ran up her arm as they touched. They grabbed their laptops and strode to the cabin's front entrance.

Tate opened the door as they stepped on the porch.

"Welcome to our abode."

Rafe grinned and leaned forward to shake hands with Tate. Tate stepped back and allowed them entry. Henry stepped into the room from another. "Hey there. The senator is sleeping now. It's been quiet and he's complaining less."

"Thanks, Henry. We've got it from here."

Henry moved to a little table near the windows and packed up his laptop. "I've researched one of the names on Wade's list. My report is in the system. I hope you both have a good night."

Henry exited the cabin, looking tired.

Tate picked up his laptop and slung it over his shoulder. "A medical kit is in the kitchen. His bandage was changed before he went to bed. He's been rather quiet. He's worried about his family. I've reassured him we have them in a safe house in Hawaii, but he'd feel better to see them. Not sure we can get them here without it being noticed, but I'll work on that."

Rafe nodded. "Thanks, Tate."

Tate nodded at her then disappeared out the front door. She opened her laptop on the little table Henry and Tate vacated. Rafe did the same.

"Do you want some water, Rafe?"

"Thanks. Yes."

She pulled two bottles of water from the refrigerator and brought them to the table. She sat across from Rafe and logged in. She grinned slightly, because it was a kick to work here with him. Side by side, so to speak. To have this in common was exciting.

...was sore, so ... pill just to get his ... used to being so sedentary. As he turned to return to his seat, headlights on the road caught his attention. He glanced at his watch and noted it was three-fifteen a.m.

"Addy. There's a car on the road."

She slowly closed her laptop case and neared the window to look down the road. She turned off the lights in the cabin and checked the lock on the door. "I'm going to check the back door lock."

He listened to her footsteps as he watched the road and driveway for any movement. His heartbeat ratcheted up, his skin prickled.

Addy entered the room once again. "I'm going out to check."

"No. We don't know if there's anyone out there or how many."

"If I catch them off guard, I have the advantage."

"Addy..."

She scrambled to the bookcase near the table they worked on. She pulled two comm units from a box and handed him one. "We can stay in touch with this. I don't want them coming near the cabin. If things start going south, call Tate."

His pulse pounded hard in his neck. His blood thrummed through his ears and sounded like a raging river. He swallowed the knot in his throat as she pulled her weapon from its holster and eased from the cabin.

He tried keeping his eyes on her, but it was dark and, in the woods, as they were, it was pitch black. Addy's breathing over their comm unit told him she was around and moving. The rustling of leaves sounded loud to him. It would sound loud to anyone outside as well. Her pace slowed and he listened for her faint breathing.

Shots sounded and he saw the blast of a gun from her area, and another from across the yard at the edge of the trees. He felt as though he'd pass out when he didn't hear anything else for a long time. Then he heard a loud thump and Addy hit the ground or something. Fighting sounded and he heard her breathing increase. She groaned as it sounded like another punch landed. A loud slap sounded. He couldn't see a thing. He looked out the window in all directions, trying in vain to see anything.

Another shot rang out and Addy's heavy breathing came over the comm unit. He hated this. He felt helpless. Out of control. Her footsteps pounding the ground was all he could hear, and finally he saw her running toward the road with the faint sliver of moonlight peeking through the trees.

A car engine started and tires on the gravel could be heard. "Shit." Was all Addy said.

He heard her feet crunching on the gravel, as she mumbled expletives to herself.

He finally saw her silhouette on the porch and opened the door for her. After she stepped inside, he twisted the lock and she pulled the comm unit from her ear.

"Bastards got away."

"How in the hell did they find us now?"

"I don't know."

He removed his comm unit and stared at his computer. "Hey, do you have the scanning software on your computer?"

"We have a portable unit on the bookcase. I saw it in the container when I pulled the comm units out."

He hurried over to the bookcase and opened the plastic container. Everything inside was well organized and he found the portable scanning device. He strode into the senator's room and scanned his body. A faint beeping sounded so he moved closer to the senator. More beeping as he neared. The senator woke, "Who's in here and what the hell are you doing?"

"It's Rafe. I need you to be quiet."

The senator huffed out a breath but was otherwise quiet. Addy padded into the room and stood silent as she watched him.

"Senator, lay on your back."

The senator huffed out a disgusted breath, but as Rafe held the portable scanner over the senator's right shoulder, the light grew bright and the beeping increased in speed.

Addy stepped forward. "Holy shit. There's a tracker in his chest."

"Dr. Krueger is compromised, Addy."

She pulled her phone out and dialed Tate. Tate answered quickly.

"Tate, Dr. Krueger placed an implant in the senator's wound."

She listened to Tate and he moved closer to the phone so he could also hear. "Take it out. I'm on my way."

"Be careful, we just had visitors and they may be lying in wait."

Tate ended the call on his end, Addy ran from the room and he looked at the senator, whose eyes were as round as beach balls.

"What does that mean?" he asked fearfully.

"It means they are still tracking you. It means Dr. Krueger is on the take and likely owned by King. And, it means we have to remove it from you or they'll continue to send people after you."

"Geez-is. Just let them have me. I'm tired of all of this. He's going to get me anyway."

"Maybe not, Senator."

Addy ran into the room with the medical kit in one hand, her phone flashlight in the other.

"I hate to turn on the lights, even though they know we're here. I don't want them seeing us clearly."

She handed her phone to Rafe after turning on the flashlight app.

"I need you to hold this over the senator while I remove the tracker."

"Oh, no. You aren't cutting me open again."

"I have no choice, Senator."

"I do!"

"No, you don't. If you want to see your family again, you need to let me remove this tracker."

She pulled items from the medical kit and laid them

on a wooden chair that stood in the corner. Pulling the chair toward the bed, she let out a long breath. "I need to do this Senator. I have some numbing ointment. And, I'll be quick."

The senator laid back and he held the phone over the senator's bandage on his chest. Addy pulled the bandage away from the wound and grimaced. "It's infected."

"Get it out of me." The senator barked.

Addy applied the numbing ointment to the senator's chest and the front door opened. She looked up at him and he moved into the living area slowly. Tate stood in the doorway, watching out the door. He turned as Rafe entered the room.

"Spencer is on his way. We'll secure the premises while Addy works on the senator."

Rafe's palms grew sweaty and he hurried into the bedroom where Addy pressed around the wound in the senator's shoulder. "I'll hurry and do no damage."

The senator only nodded once. His head flopped on the pillow and he closed his eyes.

Addy gently cut the senator's stitches. As she pulled the tissue back, the phone lite glinted off something in the senator's wound and he froze while she used a tweezers and pulled if from the senator. The tracker was the size of a ladybug. Metal in composition though now bloody.

 . . . after re . . . . The little bowl she . . . remnants of blood as she swirled the bowl to help it self-clean.

Using tweezers, she lifted the tracker from the bowl and laid it on a towel.

Tate pulled out a container for her to place the tracker in. He closed the lid to the tiny container and plugged it into his computer with a USB connection. He stared at his computer while she washed her hands.

Tate stood. "I have its ID. I'll get this to Casper and see if he can find the owner."

Rafe stepped over to his computer and sat down. "I'm here and have the same access as Casper. Let me do it."

Tate passed the information to Rafe, who went to work on his computer. Addy dried her hands and watched Rafe work. He watched his computer screen, typed information in periodically then looked up at Tate.

"It's registered to Kingsmen LLC. Kingsmen LLC is a

limited liability company whose registered agent is Natalie King. Natalie King is president-elect King's wife."

"We need to move this along faster than it's moving." Tate snapped.

Rafe huffed out a breath. "How about you and Spencer take the tracker from here and move it somewhere we can watch it. It hasn't been deactivated and they may still be regrouping and planning another visit. If you cover Spencer up as if he's a patient, and hurry him to your vehicle, then take off out of here like a bat out of hell, they may follow you. We'll effectively move them away from the senator and out into the open. Addy and I will move the senator to the HOG until we can find another place for him."

Tate glanced at Spencer. "Ready to ride?"

"Let's go."

Spencer grabbed a blanket off the back of the sofa and wrapped it around his body and covered his head. Tate took the tracker and put it in his pocket, then opened the door and helped Spencer from the cabin. Rafe locked the door behind them.

Addy sauntered to him. She smiled into his face. "It wasn't you. Do you understand? It wasn't your phone before, it was the senator."

"I did have a tracker in my phone."

"That's true. But the senator had one on him the entire time."

"Right."

She hugged him to her, squeezing him tightly and listening to his ragged breathing.

"Addy." His voice cracked when he spoke and she tilted her head up so their eyes met. "When I heard you out there fighting with them. It nearly broke me."

She grinned. "It wasn't a fight. I dropped down behind the woodpile. That's when I saw a man move across the driveway. I crawled to get a closer bead on him and he heard me. Since I'd already shot at him, he must have gotten scared and ran."

He chuckled, but it wasn't genuine. "I didn't like it. Not one bit."

"It's what I do, Rafe."

She saw his throat constrict as he swallowed. "If we're going to be together, you need to accept that."

His body expanded as he took a deep breath. "I accept it. I just didn't like it. I don't want anything bad to happen to you."

"I don't want anything bad to happen to you either, Rafe. That's why we've got to get this all sorted."

"I agree."

She rose on her toes and kissed his lips. "I'll go get the senator, enough time should have passed."

"I'll pack up our computers."

She reluctantly left Rafe in the living room and entered the bedroom where the senator's deep breathing filled the room.

"Senator." She whispered as she inched toward the bed. Shaking him lightly, "Senator. We have to leave."

"What? Why?"

"You know why. They'll figure out soon enough the tracker isn't in you and they'll come back looking for you."

He sat up, with assistance. She helped him into his shirt, then helped him with his shoes. She held his arm as he moved toward the door. Rafe held their laptops as his eyes landed on hers. He grinned slightly, then turned the lights off in the cabin and peered both ways out the door before opening the cabin door for them to exit.

Rafe moved ahead quickly and set their laptops in the backseat of the Mustang. He hurried back to them and helped the senator from the other side, to move him along quicker. They managed to get him into the passenger seat. Addy scrambled to the back seat and Rafe started it up and moved them out of the driveway.

She asked as they drove, "Senator, who in D.C. is the most upstanding person in any kind of power that can be trusted?"

"Wade Evans."

"Besides him."

The senator was quiet for a long time. "The newly elected vice president."

She took a deep breath. Casper was already working that angle. She sat back in the seat and watched out the window. The sun was just peering above the horizon emanating a red glow across the fields.

Rafe turned down the road that led to the HOG. He turned to the senator and asked, "What about the majority leader?"

Senator Jackson turned to Rafe and stared for a long time. "He's upstanding."

"Is he trustworthy?"

"I believe so. We've obviously had our differences over the years, but I've never heard a word about him being dirty."

Rafe's jaw twitched. She watched him process the information. She pulled her ID card from her back pocket and handed it to Rafe as they neared the HOG.

He pulled into her garage space, stepped from the Mustang, then reached in and held his hand out to her. She smiled, eager to take his hand once more. He pulled her from the Mustang, kissed her lips lightly, then whispered. "Take out the laptops, I'll help the senator."

"Okay."

She picked up their laptops from the back seat and stowed them over her shoulders as she watched Rafe help the senator from the vehicle and walk him into the HOG.

As she entered into the kitchen, she saw Tate sitting at the counter as Lara pulled a fresh batch of cookies from the oven.

"I thought you'd be out on the road yet."

"We tossed the tracker into the silo at the old Brown farm. Rafe is taking the senator to one of the guest rooms."

Rafe entered the kitchen and headed straight to Tate. "Can you have Gavin take me back to D.C.?"

Tate turned and looked at Rafe. What bothered her, was Rafe refused to look at her.

"Yes. What's up?"

"Casper is in hiding because of all of this. If I'm to be his replacement, it's time I step up. Too many people are being pulled into this that don't need to be. I can end it. I'll get back to my office and get word to the majority leader I need to see him privately. He's honest and he can get the ball rolling faster than trying to backdoor this. We don't have time. I have access in my office to all of the documents. I can show him what's happening. I can explain what's happened to me. And, I need to take care of firing Selisen so he doesn't cut a deal and get out. I'm tired of hiding. That's what's taking this longer to settle."

"I'll call Gavin and have him ready in an hour."

43

He stopped and stared into her beautiful face. "Because. We can't move forward while this is hanging out there. If we don't hit this bull in the middle, it'll continue to fester and lay underground. If King is sworn in, it'll never come to light. He's setting things up to keep this under wraps from keeping him with his shit choices. And, Wade, myself, and many others will lose our jobs in the process. And, we can't move forward, you and I, while this is hanging over our heads."

His heart beat wildly in his chest, his hands shook as he watched her face. Her soft lips hung open slightly. She sucked in a deep breath. "Okay."

He turned toward her and slid his hands in his pockets, mostly because he didn't want her to see him shaking. He swallowed the lump in his throat. "Addy. I've never met anyone like you. You excite me. You are smart and brave and so fucking beautiful you make me want to do better and be better. When I heard you outside this morning and thought you were fighting, a fire lit in my belly that made me realize, I need to be that for you. I have to stop running and meet this bitch head-on. It's the only way I can feel like I deserve you."

"Rafe, you do deserve..."

"No. I don't. Not yet. But I will."

He turned and finished packing his bag. He hung it on his shoulder, grabbed his laptop case and stopped in front of her. "I'll be back, when I make this right."

"You'll need protection."

"I don't think so. No one is tracking me now. I can slip into my office and get to the majority leader privately. We can get this information into his hands, secured where it's safely stored on the servers and move forward to stop the inauguration of this very corrupt president-elect."

He bent and kissed her lips. "I love you, Adelaide Masters. Remember that. And, I'll be back here soon, as a man who deserves you."

He stepped from the room before he lost his nerve. Strutting out to the kitchen, Myles sat eating Lara's cookies. "I'm your ride bro."

"Thank you, Myles."

Lara handed him a couple of cookies. "I'm sorry we've been so briefly introduced. I hope to see you again, Rafe."

"Count on it. Thank you, Lara."

He strode to the garage door, Myles close behind him and headed straight to Myles' vehicle.

He got in but held his feelings close. He'd let himself panic a bit on the plane. Then, after he had a moment of WTF, he'd set out to get his work done. He had more motivation than he ever had now that he knew what had to be done.

Myles said little on the ride except, "I told you not to hurt her."

"I told you I wouldn't."

"You think this doesn't hurt her?"

"I explained what I had to do and that I'd be back. And I will. But, I'll be a better man because of it."

"Hmm." Myles turned onto the airport property. "I wonder what the statistics are of someone promising to come back, but never coming back are?"

Rafe's jaw clenched. Myles pulled to a stop outside the hangar. Rafe opened the door and jumped from the truck. He looked in at Myles. "Why don't you give me that statistic when I return. Thanks for the ride."

He strode with his shoulders high toward the plane. Gavin stood at the bottom of the stairs waiting. "Hello, Mr. Martin. It's a good day to fly."

"Hello, Gavin. I'm happy to hear that."

He moved into the plane and sat in the seat Addy had occupied on the way here. He let his mind remember their mile high experience and let a couple of tears drop onto his cheeks.

He took a deep breath, swiped angrily at the moisture on his face, buckled his seat belt and settled in for takeoff.

Once they were safely in the air, he pulled his phone from his pocket and typed out a message to the majority leader. "I need to see you. It's urgent. It's also secret. Matter of extreme national security. Tell no one."

He swallowed the basketball-size lump in his throat and hit send. It was out there now.

He set his phone on the table and sat back to rerun through his mind what needed to happen. He debated on contacting Wade. Decided against it. If he was the next in line, he needed to act like he was already there.

His phone vibrated and he grabbed it and read the message. "I can be there this afternoon."

"See you then."

He sat back, reclined his seat and settled in for the rest of the plane ride. What he knew right now, was this was right. This was what he'd needed to do. He let himself get scared and worry about going to prison and King's power. But, he had power too. And, he'd use it. He had years of documents with King's signature all over it. He had a murder on King's record that he'd hidden. He had all the people who helped him hide it too. He'd shake this jar and pour the contents out before the entire world if that's what was needed. But, he'd do it. Then, he'd go scoop Addy up and make her his for a lifetime. Because in the end, that's what this was all about. Being the man she deserved. She was already the woman he wanted. He needed to be someone she would always be proud of.

...herself to ...she'd once told herself it ...was gross. But, she felt like Rafe had broken up with her and stomped out of the house as things got tough.

She slogged across the floor to the dresser and pulled clean clothing from inside. She woodenly moved to the bathroom and turned the water on in the shower. She ...remembered ...Rafe making love to her in her shower. She allowed herself a moment to remember how it felt when he held her close. Sucking in a lungful of air, she stepped in the shower and washed it all away. They still had the senator here and there was still work to do on their end. They'd need to clean out the safe house they'd used and remove all of their equipment. And, they needed to figure out a plan for the senator moving forward. If Rafe succeeded in bringing King down, it would bring the senator down too. So, he was facing a life in prison.

Then, there was Doctor Krueger. He needed to be dealt with too. The dirty bastard.

Stepping from the shower, she dressed, dried her hair and left the bathroom. She had a moment where she remembered Rafe sitting on her sofa waiting for her. Closing her eyes, she pulled her shoulders back and left her bedroom.

Talking in the kitchen reached her ears and she rounded the corner to see Maya, Myles, Tate, and the senator sitting at the kitchen table.

Maya smiled. "Morning."

"Morning." She glanced around at the coffee pot. Helissa stepped from the laundry room and hurried to the coffee pot. She poured Addy's coffee into her favorite mug and set it on the counter with a wink.

That led to her remembering Rafe's winks and a hard knot formed in her stomach. But she forced a smile, took her cup to the table, and sat next to Maya. "What's the topic of discussion?"

Tate nodded toward the senator. "We're discussing where the senator should stay until things are brought to light. It's likely he'll be needed to testify, so he needs to be somewhere safe. We can't trust the majority of D.C. right now to do that because King has infiltrated so many agencies, we don't know who we can trust right now."

"I was just thinking about that too."

She sipped her coffee and waited for someone else to respond.

The senator broke the silence. "I'd like to see my family."

Tate shook his head. "They're safe right now. If we bring you there, they'll be less safe. I'm sorry but that's a fact."

The senator dropped his head. "I know."

Maya sat back in her chair. "As I see it, we can keep him here. We can find another safe house for him. That splits us up for protection. Or the senator can hire a private security firm and handle his own protection."

Tate shook his head. "Casper asked us to come on this job. We're on it until Casper tells us we're off the case."

Addy sipped her coffee. "Are we cleaning out the cabin today?"

Tate nodded. "Yes. Addy, you and Maya can go out there and pack up our equipment. Then, I'll turn it over to the owner."

"Sounds good." She glanced at Maya. "Are you ready or do you need a few minutes?"

"I'm ready now. Let me go get my shoes on."

"Take a few minutes. I should check the senator's bandages."

Maya left the room and Addy went to the closet and retrieved her medical kit. She set it on the table near the senator. "Please remove your shirt, Senator."

He unbuttoned his shirt as the back door opened.

"Hi, everyone." Shianne bellowed as she entered the room. She carried bags of something and set them at the table.

"Hi, Addy. Tate." She moved to the end of the table to the senator. "You must be the man in need of new clothing. I'm Shianne, Lara's best friend. She called me this morning to do some shopping for you. I have a few things that I hope you'll like."

The senator's eyes rounded, and Addy giggled. "You can't keep wearing these dirty old clothes." She turned to Shianne. "It's nice to see you. Thank you for getting on this for us."

Shianne smiled brightly. "I love shopping. So, this made my day."

Addy grinned. "I'm about to change his bandages. Why don't you lay out the clothing and the senator can look at them afterwards. It won't take long."

"That sounds great."

Addy helped the senator remove his shirt. "I may as well toss this one." She mumbled.

The senator nodded his head and she folded the shirt and laid it on the table to set the discarded bandages on. She made quick work of removing the old bandages. Checked his wound and noted that the infection seemed to be healing. It was likely the tracker implant had caused the problem. She admired her stitches, added anti-bacterial gel and rebandaged him. Discarding the soiled bandages and shirt, Shianne took over. There would be no stopping her now. Addy grinned at Tate, who sat there looking pained to have to listen to Shianne over-explaining the quality of each piece of clothing, she left the kitchen to wash her hands and wait for Maya.

As Maya left her bedroom and moved toward her she stopped dead. She mouthed, "Is that Shianne?"

Addy nodded and Maya closed her eyes. They all liked Shianne. She was a wonderful person. But, when you got her talking about clothing, she would go on and on and on.

Maya grabbed Addy's arm and swiftly pulled her to the kitchen and to the garage door.

"See you later. We're off to work." Maya quipped.

They slipped out the door before Shianne finished describing the tweed in this year's new slacks.

...ped quietly

...Leesha startled as

...in the office please."

He continued on to his office, set his computer case on the desk and the instant Leesha appeared he said, "Close the door please."

She did as he asked. He noticed the large swallow she ...before... ...and his desk...

"Please sit."

She sat on the edge of the chair, her spine was stiff, her hands in her lap.

"Leesha. I need to know everything you know about Brett Selisen."

Leesha burst out in tears, her face in her hands. Rafe's brows furrowed and he pulled a tissue from the box on the corner of his desk and handed it across the desk to her.

"Leesha. Please. We need to chat about this."

Leesha took the proffered tissue and dabbed at her

eyes and nose. Her lips still quivered, and Rafe took a deep breath.

"So, apparently some things have been going on that I'm not aware of. Please tell me."

Leesha swallowed a few times. She inhaled a deep breath and let it out slowly. "Brett and I were dating. He wanted to keep it quiet. I was happy to comply. I don't think..."

Tears spilled again. Rafe waited patiently.

Leesha took a deep breath again. "I don't think he liked me as a girlfriend. I think he may have been using me for access to you."

"That's why you let him drop the Distible documents in my office rather than you bringing them in?"

"Yes." She dabbed her eyes. "After you asked about it I thought it was a weird question. Then, all the weird things happening. You leaving town. I heard your house was broken into. And now Brett is in jail. It hit me that some, if not all, of this has to be related."

Rafe pinched his lips together. "He installed a tracker on my phone while he was in here."

"Oh my god. I'm so sorry. I promise you I had no idea. I'm so sorry Mr. Martin."

He held his hands up. "Leesha, it's alright. You're not the first person to be taken advantage of. I've always felt I could trust you. I need to know right here and now that I can. My life depends on it."

Her eyes rounded as she looked at him. "You can trust me. I'm so sorry this happened."

He swallowed. "Right now, Leesha. I need you to wait in your office for the majority leader. It's a secret meeting and no one, and I mean, no one, can know we're meeting. Do you understand?"

"Yes sir."

"Okay."

She stood. "I'm so sorry Mr. Martin."

He held his hand up again. "Leesha, please. You're about to prove to me how reliable you are."

"Okay."

She left his office and he logged into his computer, then the secret server he and Casper used. As he waited, every time Addy crossed his mind, which was nearly always, he pushed it away. He needed to do this. He needed to get this done.

His phone buzzed. "Mr. Martin, the majority leader, Mr. Andrews, is here."

"Send him in please."

Rafe stood to greet Andrews, his guts tightened, and his palms were sweaty. Everything rode on this.

The door opened and Mr. Andrews entered the room. He was tall, with sandy colored hair, and deep blue eyes. Rafe knew he was in his late forties, had been a rising star in the political arena for a couple of years now, and had always been nice to chat with.

Walking around his desk, Rafe held his hand out. "Robert, it's nice to see you and thank you for coming on short notice."

"It's nice to see you, Rafe. I understand Wade has been out for a bit now."

"Yes. It's what I'd like to talk to you about."

He held his hand out to Andrews to take a seat, then walked around his desk and sat. He folded his hands on his desk. Mostly to keep them from shaking. "Robert, what I'm about to share with you is incredible. And it will set precedent and change this country forever. I'm sorry to have to lay this at your feet, but since you are the majority leader and will be in this upcoming term as well, you're the only person to handle this."

Robert shifted in his chair and took a deep breath. "Okay."

Rafe took a deep breath. "I have proof in the form of documents and witnesses, that our newly elected president has been dealing oil for arms with Yerezdan. And, during those dealings, the chief of staff for the prime minister of Yerezdan found out about the deals and threatened to expose them. President-elect King sent a group over to have a chat with the chief of staff, Mr. Bertrum Malachi, and during that chat, Mr. Malachi was murdered. Further, the cabinet the president-elect is putting in place all have ties to Yerezdan."

Robert sat back in his seat and stared at Rafe. His mouth dropped open slightly as he processed the information. He finally closed his eyes briefly, shook his head and opened them again. He stared into Rafe's eyes. "What proof do you have?"

Rafe turned his laptop around and showed him some of the documents. "Senator Pierce Jackson is the witness. He personally carried documents to and from Yerezdan for King. He received payment for smuggling these documents from then Senator King. We have the bank records showing payments. We have the death certificate from Mr. Malachi showing the date and time, and the cause of death is murder. At this time, we have the travel records of the men who went over to Yerezdan to speak with the chief of staff when he suddenly was murdered."

"Senator Jackson is complicit. Is he saying he'll testify?"
"He will."

"This is...my god. What are the other documents?"

"I have access to the contracts signed by Senator King

agreeing to send over arms for oil. The oil was what Senator King professed to have helped the United States procure when he was pushing his no-drilling agenda saying we had 'reserves' and didn't need to drill."

"What are you...wait..." Robert Andrews shook his head. "Senator Jackson lost his re-election bid."

"Yes. He believes King set it up that way to get him out of the way."

"Why?"

"He was finished with him. I happen to know King infiltrated my office to keep an eye on things. One of my aides, who is now in jail for bank fraud, was spying for King. He placed a tracker on my phone to keep me in his sites. This was after Senator Jackson came to Wade Evans to tell him what happened. Wade had to go dark because of threats to his family."

"What?"

"I was also under personal attack. Selisen, my former aide, planted blood in my house to make it look like I murdered someone. I believe they were going to use that to blackmail me into giving up Wade. I am also a witness to the fact that several attempts have been made to kill Senator Jackson. And he's been shot in the shoulder as a result. He's now in a safe house."

Robert sat for a long time processing this information. He took deep breaths as the gravity of what he'd just heard sank in. After a few minutes, he finally said, "We can't let him be sworn in."

[illegible] Maya did [illegible] out of curiosity. Addy [illegible] where she'd hidden very early this morning to see what it looked like in the daytime. She found the woodpile, though she wasn't sure how she'd found it before. It was tucked in the crook between a clump of bushes and the woods. The pile was only four feet high or so but it was only about two feet wide. God [illegible] She followed the driveway to the road and looked from that angle to see that the house couldn't be seen from here. Though at night, with the lights on inside, it was a possibility it was seen through the trees. She found a drop of blood near the edge of the driveway and squatted down to take a closer look. A few inches away there was another drop of blood and a place where the gravel had been disturbed by someone's hand. It definitely wasn't a shoe or foot and more blood was smeared into the gravel.

"What are you looking at?" Maya asked.

"Last night, or early this morning rather, we had a

visitor out here. It's what made us aware there was a tracker on the senator. For a while, I thought maybe the senator was playing us. I was pissed and went in to scan him. I remember shooting at whoever it was when I saw something glint on his chest. He shot back, and I ducked behind the woodpile. He fell around here, I think." She pointed to the gravel. There's blood up there, and over here, suggesting I shot him."

"It was self-defense."

"I know. But, I'm surprised he took off is all. If he was hired to do a job, why did he cut and run? He didn't come after me."

"Maybe you surprised him."

"Right, but a hired killer is a hired killer. They know the risk. They normally aren't scared off so easily."

"That's true." Maya walked along the edge of the driveway looking for anything that seemed weird.

Addy moved across the driveway where the man was in hiding looking for anything that might shed some light on who it was. She found the shell casing from his bullet. Nothing special about it. A nine-millimeter, which is what she used.

"Nine mil?" Maya asked.

"Yeah."

"Nothing else?"

"No. I just thought maybe I'd find something. It's been bothering me."

Maya stood near her, saying nothing, just letting her think it out. But, she softly said, "Maybe he wasn't a hired killer."

"As in?"

"As in, he's just someone who thought he could do it.

A petty criminal. Some lowlife paid to do something with no ties to anyone in particular and easy to discard."

Addy swallowed. "Like Jensen Gable."

Maya nodded. "Maybe there are airline records or car rental records here. Maybe Piper can dig into Jensen Gable's bank records and find gas receipts or something."

"That's a great idea."

Addy hurried to Maya's Jeep and got in. Her cousin jumped in the driver's seat with a grin on her face. "Glad to see some spunk back in you girl."

She turned to Maya and the tears formed instantly. "I love him."

"I know."

Maya started her Jeep and led them toward the HOG. Addy stared out the window the entire ride home, grateful for Maya's silence, but also her presence. They were more like sisters than cousins and when it came to support, she looked for Maya first. Myles too, but Maya first.

After she'd pulled into the garage, Maya reached over and squeezed her hand. "He'll be back."

Her lip quivered. "I hope so."

Maya squeezed her hand again. "Let's go get busy. It'll take your mind off of Rafe for a while. Baby steps."

"Baby steps."

"And bonus. Shianne has left."

Addy giggled, swiped at her tears and climbed out of the Jeep. She walked to the back and they started pulling their equipment totes from the back. After getting some things inside, she'd repack the totes so they were ready for their next mission. By that time, it'd be bedtime and maybe she'd be tired enough to sleep.

After unloading the totes, she entered the house and went to Tate's office.

"Hey, Addy. How is the house?"

"It's cleaned out. You can turn it over."

"Will do."

Addy sat in one of the chairs in Tate's office.

"What else?" He asked.

"Maya and I took a closer look at the area where the assailant was this morning. I found blood in the driveway. I must have hit him when I shot. It also looked like he fell, and maybe the palm of his hand is ripped up from the gravel in the driveway. I found an area where there was blood pushed into the gravel."

"Okay." Tate stopped looking at his computer and gave her his full attention.

"He left a job he was hired to do. A hired killer only leaves once he's completed his job or killed himself. Which made me think of Jensen Gable. He is suspected of carving up Rafe's locker at the gym, setting the explosive off and has been in the wind since then. What if he's here? He's a petty criminal, not used to doing the big stuff, but they could have blackmailed him to come here and kill the senator."

Tate's brows rose into his hair. "Good thinking, Addy."

"So, if Piper could dig into his bank records and locate some receipts. Gas, car rental, airplane tickets. Something to lead us to him."

"I'll call right now."

"Thanks, Tate. If there's anything I need to do, please let me know. Otherwise, I'll be out repacking the totes."

Tate chuckled. "Thanks, Addy."

She left Tate's office feeling revived. Maybe she helped after all.

47

Robert [...] could go home or [...] was about to go down. He shared the documents with Andrews via copying them to a thumb drive. Andrews' hands were shaking as he left the office, knowing what he had to do. He told Rafe to stay put and that had been three hours ago.

Rafe picked up his phone and called Tate.

"Before the details come in?"

"I've given everything to majority leader Robert Andrews. He was visibly shaken and left the office with a thumb drive filled with evidence. I'd say, tighten security around the senator. Shit will get real very soon."

"Thanks for calling, Rafe. I appreciate the heads-up."

He hung up from Tate and sat on the large leather sofa in his office and dialed Addy. He missed the hell out of her. It felt worse because he was so far away from her now. He felt emotionally far from her too after the way he left this morning.

"Hi, Rafe. How are you?"

"Addy. Honey, I miss the hell out of you. How are you?"

He heard her sniff lightly and take a deep breath. "I'm fine. I've been staying busy. How are you?"

"I'm here in my office at seven at night waiting for Robert Andrews to let me know what's happened. I don't know if I can go home. And, for now, I'm safe here, so I'm staying put. I miss you and wish I could hold you right now."

"I wish you could hold me too. Did you mean it? You're coming back?"

"Of course I meant it."

A knock on his office door startled him. "Hey baby, someone's at my door. I'll let you know what's going on in a little while."

He stood from the sofa and sucked in a lungful of air. He dialed Robert Andrew's phone and waited for him to answer.

"Rafe. I'm at your office door."

"Are you alone?"

"Yes."

Rafe's knees shook as he walked across the floor of his office. It had never felt so large. He opened the door and saw Andrews standing there, alone and visibly shaken.

He opened the door wider, "Come in."

He closed and locked the door behind Andrews. Andrews shuffled to the chairs in front of Rafe's desk and plopped down. Rafe took the vacant chair next to him.

"What's happening?"

"I've told a small caucus of our party what I have. We're researching right now what needs to be done. This is unprecedented. The Supreme Court has never ruled on an indictment of a sitting president and likely will not, due to the unique powers the president holds. But King isn't president yet, so we don't have much time. We're working on an indictment now. It will be taken to the DOJ in the morning. I'm sure King will hear about it before that happens. We know there are spies everywhere and this is big."

"Yes. That's a fact."

Andrews leaned forward. "Rafe. I mean this with all sincerity. Get out of town. Go somewhere until this blows over. As soon as King finds out, he'll be angrier than a wet hornet and he will lash out. After reading some of the documents over, his life is on the line here. He'll go to prison for a long time and he won't do well there. Get out. There's nothing you can do from here that you can't do from somewhere else."

"Are you sure?"

"Yes. Go. Go now. Don't look back. I'll keep in touch. I bought a burner phone." His hands shook as he pulled a burner phone from his inside pocket. It was still in the package and sealed.

"I have this number." He handed him a phone number with a shaking hand. "My burner phone. I'll contact you on this."

"Thank you, Robert. I appreciate the heads-up."

"Do you have transportation? Can you get out of town without notice?"

"Yes. I believe so."

Andrews stood. They shook hands and he hurriedly left Rafe's office. Rafe packed up his computer and swiftly left the building via the secret hall. He started to order an Uber on his phone, then worried that would be a record. He decided to walk to the street outside of the parking area and get on a bus. No one would look for him on a public bus.

The entire walk he looked around him, checked his surroundings and basically felt like a man on the run, which he sort of was. He found the bus stop, waited in the shadows rather than the lighted glassed-in bus stop and continued to look around, trying not to look suspicious.

Just before the bus came rolling up, a taxi stopped and he ran to the taxi. He got into the back seat and gave the cab driver the address to the Bowman home. His vehicle was there. From there, he'd drive to Kentucky and Addy. It was an eight-hour drive, eight and a half with gas stops. He'd be there by five in the morning barring issues.

He sat quietly in the back of the cab, he watched as Washington D.C. sped past his window and he wondered why he wanted to live here. It was filled with criminals and spies. He didn't want to associate with either. Yet a couple of weeks ago, he was proud as hell of himself for living here. For rising to the top. But the top of a pile of shit is...shit.

The cab driver dropped him in front of the Bowman home, he paid with cash, a large tip for the cab driver that would hopefully buy him silence should anyone ask.

He brusquely walked through the backyard, got to the garage, and wondered how he'd get inside. The house was dark, Catalina was gone for the day. He called Addy.

"Hi, Rafe. What's going on?"

"I'm at the Bowman's to get my vehicle, but I don't know how to open the garage door. Any ideas for me?"

She was quiet for a moment, then the door began to open. "I have the garage door programed into my phone now. Did it open?"

"It did. Thank you."

"What happened with Andrews?"

"He's putting things in motion. I have to lay low."

"Okay."

"Let me call you later. I want to get out of here."

"Let me stay on until you back out. I'll close the door."

He hurried around the garage and jumped into his vehicle. He started it up and backed out slowly. "Okay. Close the door."

He watched as the door slid shut.

"Where are you staying tonight?"

"On the road."

"Rafe..."

"Hey, baby, I promise. It's all good. Can I call you later? I want to focus so I can get out of town without being seen."

"Of course. Drive carefully, Rafe."

"I will. I'll talk to you later on."

He ended the call. His gut twisted but he wanted to surprise her.

had been so ... on edge. She'd ... call and he didn't. She got out ... went to the bathroom and took a long shower.

Leaving her room, dressed, somewhat refreshed, and a bit hungry, she went straight to the kitchen. Helissa was making breakfast. She looked at her watch and saw it was seven forty. She'd slept later than she thought.

"Good morning, Ms. Addy."

"Good morning, Helissa. As usual, everything smells so good."

"Thank you, Ms. Addy."

Helissa set a cup of coffee in front of her and Addy sat at the counter. "Did everyone eat already?"

"Mr. Vickers, Mr. Lawson, and Mr. Sager have eaten."

She giggled. "You know you can call us by our first names."

Helissa smiled and stirred something in the frying pan.

"What about the senator?"

"I haven't seen him this morning."

"Thank you. I'll go check on him."

She went to the closet and picked up her medical kit, then headed across the living room toward the bedroom the senator was using. She knocked on the door and listened but didn't hear anything.

"Senator?"

She knocked again then twisted the knob. She peered inside and his bed was unmade and empty. She took a walk around the building to the other bedrooms but didn't see the senator anywhere.

Poking her head in Tate's office, she found that empty as well. Taking a deep breath she padded across the floor to Maya's room. She knocked a couple of times and heard Maya say, "Come in."

Opening the door she saw her cousin, pulling her hair up into a ponytail at the top of her head.

"Hey, what's up?"

"Where is everyone? Helissa said Tate, Myles, and Spencer had eaten. I went to check on the senator and he's gone. Tate's not in his office. It seems like it's just you and me."

"Hmm. I don't know. Let's get a cup of coffee and go in search of them."

Maya strutted across the floor, Addy followed her not feeling nearly as peppy. Maybe she should have had her coffee first before going on this scavenger hunt.

They entered the kitchen and Helissa had a cup of coffee sitting out for Maya, and hers had been topped off. It was easy to get spoiled here.

Maya smiled. "Thank you, Helissa. You're the best person in this house."

"Hey, ouch." Addy tapped Maya's shoulder.

Helissa laughed and Maya put her arm around Addy's shoulders. "Let's go outside and see how many vehicles are in the garage."

They stepped into the garage, Tate's vehicle was there, Myles' was gone, Spencer's was there. Lara's SUV was gone. Kenna's car was gone. Three of the garage doors were open.

They walked out to the backyard and saw Tate carrying Barrett in a blanket. He stopped at the trees and showed the little guy leaves and branches.

Spencer came out of the shooting range and moved toward them. "What are you two doing?"

Maya turned to look at Spencer. "Looking at Tate and Barrett. Can you believe he has a baby?"

Spencer chuckled. "Yeah. It's something."

Maya sipped her coffee. Addy did the same. Spencer's stomach growled. "I'm hungry. I'll see you at the breakfast table."

"You just ate."

"Not enough."

Maya nodded. "I'm hungry too. Come on Addy, let's eat and see what we're going to do today."

Addy shook her head. "Where's the senator?"

Spencer stopped walking into the house. "Isn't he in his room?"

"No. I went in to change his bandages and he wasn't there."

Spencer glanced around the backyard and didn't see the senator anywhere. Maya shook her head.

Addy began feeling alarmed. She hustled back into the kitchen. "Helissa, did you see the senator at all this morning?"

"No, Ms. Addy."

Spencer stalked across the living room to the senator's room. He came back out a few moments later. "His clothes are all still here."

Tate and Barrett entered the kitchen, Tate cooing at Barrett. He froze when he saw them all staring. "What's going on?"

Addy shook her head. "The senator is gone."

"What do you mean gone?"

"Gone as in he isn't here in the HOG."

"Did you look in the gun range and workout room?"

Spencer replied, "I just came from the gun range and he isn't in there. I highly doubt he's in the workout room."

Addy hustled to the door. "I'll go look though, just in case."

She hurried to the workout room, swung open the door and the lights flickered on. No one was in the room. Her stomach rolled. There was absolutely no way anyone had come into their home and taken him. One of them would have heard something. Breeching the gate would have set off all kinds of alarms. She hurried back to the house. "He's not out there."

Tate hurried to his office, Barrett in tow. Addy tried to think of anywhere the senator could be. On a whim, she went back out to the garage and looked in each vehicle parked in there. She'd checked her vehicle, Maya's Jeep, Spencer's truck, Tate's truck, and even Helissa's vehicle in the driveway.

Her stomach began to sour. They were responsible. It never occurred to any of them that he could be taken from here. She turned to go back inside when tires crunched on the gravel near the road. The hum of the gates sliding open reached her ears and she waited to see if the senator had gone with Myles somewhere. That could absolutely have happened.

The vehicle that turned toward the back of the HOG wasn't Myles' truck though. She blinked a few times in case she was seeing an illusion. The vehicle stopped behind her car. She stood straight, her stomach knotted tightly.

The driver's door opened and Rafe exited his SUV. He looked tired. He had a couple days growth of beard, which looked amazing on him. He strode toward her slowly. His steps were deliberate. His eyes never looked from hers.

He stopped just a few inches from her. She stared into his eyes. He looked tired. The darkness under them a tell-tale sign he'd been up all night. Then it dawned on her. "Did you drive all night to get here?"

"Yes."

"Rafe. Why didn't you tell me?"

"I wanted to surprise you."

"Rafe." A sob broke from her throat and she stepped toward him. He held his hand out to stop her.

"Addy." He took a deep breath. "I told you I'd come back and be someone who you deserved and I'd be worthy enough to deserve you. I've done what I could do. The rest will take some time to show whether what I did worked or not. But, what I do know is this. I love you, Adelaide Masters. I want to be with you all of my days."

He knelt down on one knee. "Adelaide Masters, you've enamored me from the moment I met you. You've made me realize I don't want to be alone the rest of my life. I want to spend my days making you proud and happy. Will you marry me?"

She swallowed, another sob broke from her throat and she was afraid to move. Her knees shook, her whole body was shaking. "Rafe." She swallowed the lump in her throat and let the tears fall. "Yes. I am proud of you. I am so in love with you it hurts. So, yes, I'll marry you."

He stood and scooped her up in his arms. She wrapped her arms around his neck and cried into the crook of his neck. He squeezed her tightly to his body. After a few moments he let her slide down his body. He reached into his pocket and pulled a small velvet box from inside. "I stopped this morning at a jewelry store in Brook-side. If this isn't what you'd like, we'll find one together. But, I thought this fit you perfectly."

He opened the box and the ring inside was a stunner. Beautiful, sparkling and, he was right, it was perfect. A diamond band, graced with a large square cut diamond on top. She'd wear it proudly forever.

EPILOGUE

her ... He asked ... to finish talking in the

Maya leaned over. "Are you sure you don't know what's going on in there?"

"I'm sure. They've been working on something secret all week."

M[...] Aunt Iris and Uncle Josh were coming today."

Addy looked at her watch, which graced her left wrist, and also allowed her to look once again at her gorgeous engagement ring. "They should be here in an hour."

The office door opened and Rafe stepped toward the conference room first, then Tate moved toward them. They were grinning and looked like two men with a secret. Rafe's eyes met hers and his lips turned up slightly in a smile. They entered the conference room. Rafe sat next to her. He winked at her when he sat, and as always, that just did something to her.

Tate cleared his throat. "So, first of all, thank you all for coming. As you know, Rafe and I have been working out some details that we weren't ready to share with you until now. As you know, Rafe is taking over Wade's position as Casper. We've been having phone conferences with Casper to work out how this might look. Rafe, do you want to finish?"

Rafe sat forward. "Sure. Thank you. I'm leaving the Department effective immediately." He glanced at her and smiled. She knew he was planning on leaving there. The sheer level of deception surrounding being Casper was more than he cared to deal with moving forward. "I've already informed them of my departure. Wade has already given his notice of retirement as well. Under the circumstances with the threat of harm surrounding both of us, we're being given nice settlement packages. I'm taking the work Wade has done with teams such as yours, and others, private. That means, I don't have to hide from the Department what I'm doing to set up operations. It's likely still not legal, but you and teams like you are necessary.

Tate has offered me office space here at the HOG, which I am happily accepting. It'll take me a little bit to set up and get back in business, but Wade and I have all of our contacts from years of work, and we'll be letting them know how to reach me. The Department doesn't know about any of that business and we've already copied over our private server to a new server here on site."

He reached over and took her hand in his. Maya turned and gave her a look. "Liar."

"I wasn't allowed to say anything."

Maya punched her in the arm. "I'm proud of you."

Spencer looked across the table. "Congratulations, Rafe. That's great news."

Henry reached over and shook Rafe's hand. Myles did the same thing. Maya looked past her to Rafe. "Congratulations and welcome to the family, Rafe. We're happy to have you."

"Thank you, Maya."

He leaned over and kissed Addy's lips. "Congratulations," she offered.

Rafe grinned. "Our first order of business is locating the senator. As you know, we believe he climbed into the back of Myles' truck and hid. That got him past cameras and security. We did find blood in the back of Myles' truck. He's likely opened up his wound climbing back there. He'd been complaining he wanted to be with his family, he may have felt he'd find them on his own. I'm not sure. But, he's out there and we need him to testify. We have to find him before King does."

Rafe continued. "Give me a couple of hours and I'll have some places for us to check out. In the meantime, if you'd all check airline check ins, bus stations, area car services, etc. That may help us narrow down places to begin physically searching."

Maya nodded. "I'll take airlines."

Myles responded, "I'll take buses."

Spencer grinned. "I'm on car services."

Henry chuckled. "I'll take train stations."

Tate nodded. "Great. Thanks everyone. We're using the room near the front door. Henry's old room is Rafe's office. We've got the server in there and computers set up. He has a few more pieces of furniture to bring in, and he'll be ready to go."

Everyone stood to go get their computers. Rafe stood

and placed his hand on her shoulder. "Can we have a word?"

"Of course."

She stood and exited the conference room first, Rafe close behind her. They stepped into his new office, and she grinned. "It's coming along nicely."

"It sure is." He closed the door. "I want to ask you something, and all I'm asking is for you to think about it."

"Okaaay." Fear raced through her body.

He grinned. "It isn't bad. At least I don't think it is."

"Just tell me Rafe."

"We're getting married. That stands to reason we'll have children one day. When you're pregnant, I gotta be honest and say I'm not going to like you being out on a mission, fighting, being shot at, and all the other stuff with you pregnant. I don't like it now, but I know it's what you do and you're good at it. Very good at it. But, I'd like you to consider working with me in the company. As we get back up to speed, I'll need someone like you, with intimate knowledge of all that's involved in a mission to coordinate tactics, equipment, and contacts."

Addy stared into his eyes. "I hadn't thought of that. I don't like not being out there working with my team."

"As I said, it's something to think about."

She stepped forward and kissed his lips. "I'll think about it. Absolutely. And, if there are missions I want to participate in, I'll have the freedom to do that?"

His smile was magnetic. "Yes, all I ask, is for you to think about it. And, yes, of course if there are missions you want to participate in, you have the freedom to do that."

"Okay. And, what about Leesha? Is she alright after all of this change?"

He grinned. "She's staying there to work with the new

special counsel and she's going to be my contact there, should I need something I don't have access to. She said she feels like a secret agent now and in her words, 'That's pretty badass.'"

She laughed. "Good for her. Now, we have to get ready for my parents to visit."

Rafe hid his face with his hands. "Oh, no, I'd forgotten about that."

She laughed. "You so did not."

He held her close. "No, I didn't. I'm excited to meet them."

"Good. They'll be here shortly."

"Okay. What do we have to do to get ready?"

A knock sounded on the door and Rafe squeezed her once, then loosened his arms and let her step back. "Come in."

Maya appeared in the doorway. "Sorry to bother you. I just got a weird call that someone fitting the senator's description was seen up in Hickory Hills. I'm heading up there to check it out. Myles is coming with me. Please tell Aunt Isi and Uncle Josh we'll see them later."

Addy nodded. "Good luck Maya. Call me if you need anything."

Maya chuckled. "Right. Auntie Isi would kick my ass if I took you away when they first get here."

"I feel responsible though."

"We all do. We'll be back as soon as we check out the sighting."

Thank you so much for reading Guarding Adelaide. Rafe and Addy were fun to write and they are such a good pair.

I am so fortunate to be able to do what I love - write. It's because of you. I have so many stories running through my head and so many ideas bubbling up inside I can't wait to get them on paper (you know, or computer) for you. So, thank you for allowing me to do what I love.

But, now Maya is about to meet Jasiah Weston, a member of the BRR, though they no longer call themselves that. And, where on earth did Senator Jackson go? Is Wade still Casper? These questions are answered in Shielding Maya.

Get your copy of Shielding Maya direct from me at - https://www.pjfiala.com/product/shielding-maya-pb/

ACKNOWLEDGMENTS

Throughout writing the GHOST Legacy series, I've asked my Road Queens to name characters, places, and businesses. They've responded with wonderful names! Below are all the contributions to the GHOST Legacy characters, places and businesses and the lovely readers who were so creative and generous to have named them.

Reader who named	Character	Description	Book
Abigail Capps	Paxton's General Store	Grocery Store in Glen Hollow	1 - Finding Lara
Amy Barber	Fort Abraham	Army base constructed in Glen Hollow	1 - Finding Lara
Anne Walker	Lara's Delights	Lara's Bakery	1 - Finding Lara
Beckie Johnson Lowe	Chestnut Grove	Furniture Store in Glen Hollow	1 - Finding Lara
Becky Johnson Lowe	Brayden Lowe	BRR Council Member	1 - Finding Lara
Belinda Jackson Hercule	Sharon Jackson	Laylah Bennit's Best Friend	1 - Finding Lara
Elinda Moody	Keaton Bennit	Lara's Father/Police Officer	1 - Finding Lara
Ginna Honeycutt	Cole Honeycutt	BRR Council Member	1 - Finding Lara
Jamie Rogers	Black Road Resistance (BRR)		1 - Finding Lara
Jayne Smith	Craig Howard	BRR Vice President	1 - Finding Lara
Jo West	Jasiah Weston	BRR Member	1 - Finding Lara
Jo West	Baxter Fenshaw	Construction Manager	1 - Finding Lara
Jo West	Bloomin' Lovely	Flower Shoppe in Glen Hollow	1 - Finding Lara
Julia Murphy	Alan	Paxton's employee	1 - Finding Lara
Julie Ann Price	Liam Price	BRR Treasurer	1 - Finding Lara
Karen Cranford LeBeau	Klaire Brown	Shianne's Mom	1 - Finding Lara
Karen Cranford LeBeau	Millie LeBeau	Bourbon Ball Conference Chair	1 - Finding Lara
Karen Cranford LeBeau	Sheriff Rx Cranford	Glen Hollow Sheriff	1 - Finding Lara
Karen Cranford LeBeau	Brenner Matthews	BRR Teen	1 - Finding Lara
Karen Cranford LeBeau	Ramsay Stewart	BRR Teen	1 - Finding Lara
Kathy Franklin	Hickory Hills	Hickory Hills Kentucky	1 - Finding Lara
Kim Kurtz	Glen Hollow	Glen Hollow Kentucky	1 - Finding Lara
Kristi Hombs Kopydlowski	Lara Bennit	Heroine in Finding Lara	1 - Finding Lara
Kristi Hombs Kopydlowski	Troy Brown	Shianne's Father	1 - Finding Lara
Lisa Mansfield	Reece Mansfield	BRR Council Member	1 - Finding Lara
Mary Lou Melzer	Kent Bennit	Lara's half-brother	1 - Finding Lara
Monique Mosseau Westwood	Brookswood	Nearest town to Glen Hollow	1 - Finding Lara
Nancy Hoch	Homemade in the Hollow	Diner in Glen Hollow	1 - Finding Lara
Nathalie Juergensen	Hairy Beards	Barber Shop in Glen Hollow	1 - Finding Lara
Nicky Ortiz	Porter's Steakhouse	Fine Dinning in Glen Hollow	1 - Finding Lara
Nicky Ortiz	Devine Designs	Shianne's Clothing boutique	1 - Finding Lara
Pamela Reveal	Matthew Vickers	Tate's Brother	1 - Finding Lara
Ronda Barnes-Howard	Everett Howard	BRR President	1 - Finding Lara
Sally Harris	Brook Harris	BRR Council	1 - Finding Lara
Terra Oenning	Rayleigh Winters	Glen Hollow Mayor	1 - Finding Lara
Terri DeMario	Flynn DeMario	Owner of Gas Station	1 - Finding Lara
Tjuana TJ Brown	Shianne Brown	Lara's Best Friend	1 - Finding Lara
Yolanda Tobiasen	Laylay Bennit	Lara's Mother	1 - Finding Lara

Amy Ball	The Stitchery	Prospective name for the HOG	2 - Saving Elena
Anna Marie Flamini	Amelia	Elena's childhood friend	2 - Saving Elena
Arlene Miklovic	Liliana Weston	Gerard Weston's wife/mother of Jasiah	2 - Saving Elena
Belinda Jackson Hercule	Elena Dorsey (last name)	Heroine of Saving Elena	2 - Saving Elena
Cathy Christmas	Helissa	HOG housekeeper and cook	2 - Saving Elena
Dana Zamora	Sown Home	Prospective name for the HOG	2 - Saving Elena
Deb Jones Diem	Hemmed In	Prospective name for the HOG	2 - Saving Elena
Debbie Zsidai	Elenor	Medicine woman for the BRR	2 - Saving Elena
Gail Whitley	Needle Point	Prospective name for the HOG	2 - Saving Elena
Ginna Honeycutt	Carter Gordon	Police Officer	2 - Saving Elena
Jayne Smith	Craig Howard	President of the BRR	2 - Saving Elena
Jayne Smith	Theresa	Elenor's (medicine woman) daughter	2 - Saving Elena
Jessica Zoe	Grace Dorsey	Elena's Mother	2 - Saving Elena
Jo West	Jasiah Weston	Gerard Weston's son	2 - Saving Elena
Julia Murphy	Zipped Tight	Prospective name for the HOG	2 - Saving Elena
Karen Cranford LeBeau	Button Down	Prospective name for the HOG	2 - Saving Elena
Kathy Franklin	Hickory Hills	Hickory Hills Kentucky	2 - Saving Elena
Kerry Harteker	Mending Box	Prospective name for the HOG	2 - Saving Elena
Kerry Harteker	Elena's mom's health Issues		2 - Saving Elena
Kim Kurtz	Glen Hollow Kentucky	Glen Hollow Kentucky	2 - Saving Elena
Liz Bradley	Maria Bradley	Police Officer in Glen Hollow	2 - Saving Elena
Lyne Carroll	Elena Dorsey (first name)	Heroine of Saving Elena	2 - Saving Elena
Lynne Kerr	Gerard Weston	Vice President of the BRR	2 - Saving Elena
Marlene Davis	Hanalore Howard	Craig's Wife	2 - Saving Elena
Nicky Ortiz	HOG (Home Office Garage)	The sewing factory the GHOST team converted to their headquarters	2 - Saving Elena
Abigail Capps	Squeaky Clean Laundromat	Laundromat in Glen Hollow	3 - Rescuing Kenna
Alana Ackerman	Rhys	Dani's fiance (Dani is Spencer's sister)	3 - Rescuing Kenna
Beckie Johnson Lowe	Colt Lowe	Kenna's former boyfriend	3 - Rescuing Kenna
Cindy Pearson	Ami Pearson	Colt Lowe's fiance	3 - Rescuing Kenna
Dana Zamora	Sean and Jonathon Lawrence	Kenna's brothers	3 - Rescuing Kenna
Elizabeth Ward Sadowsky	Chesson Ward	Owner of the Broken Barrel Saloon	3 - Rescuing Kenna
Jayne Smith	Attorney Francesca Smith	Attorney in Glen Hollow	3 - Rescuing Kenna
Julia Murphy	Attorney Peter Murphy	Attorney in Glen Hollow	3 - Rescuing Kenna
Julia Murphy	Alan		3 - Rescuing Kenna
Killaine Kennedy	Niya Lawrence	Kenna's Mother	3 - Rescuing Kenna
Kim Kurtz	Howie Lawrence	Kenna's Father	3 - Rescuing Kenna
Monique Mousseau	Spencer Lawson	Hero in Rescuing Kenna	3 - Rescuing Kenna
Nathalie Juergensen	Daniel Juergensen	Co-Owner of Networking Solutions	3 - Rescuing Kenna
Nicky Ortiz	Lady Liberty Law Office	Law Office in Glen Hollow	3 - Rescuing Kenna
Nicky Ortiz	The Paper Trail	Kenna's process service business	3 - Rescuing Kenna
Peggy Fowler	Kenna Lawrence (first name)	Heroine in Rescuing Kenna	3 - Rescuing Kenna
Sharon R. Cowan	Kenna Lawrence (last name)	Heroine in Rescing Kenna	3 - Rescuing Kenna

Arlene Miklovic	Lady	Horse	4 - Protecting Everleigh
Cay Krueger Scheumack	Zahn Krueger	President of the Town Council	4 - Protecting Everleigh
Dana Zamora	Zander Zamora	Real Estate Agent	4 - Protecting Everleigh
Debbie Zsidai	Dr. Emily Zsidai	Veteranarian in Glen Hollow	4 - Protecting Everleigh
Holli Kohls	Harper	Horse	4 - Protecting Everleigh
Kim Kurtz	Geoffrey Kurtz	Farmer in Glen Hollow	4 - Protecting Everleigh
Kristi Malloy	Zachary Malloy	Singer	4 - Protecting Everleigh
Marie Evans	Case Evans	Abusive Farmer	4 - Protecting Everleigh
Marlene Davis	Sallie	Horse	4 - Protecting Everleigh
Michelle Terry	Diamond	Horse	4 - Protecting Everleigh
Monique Mousseau Westwood	Sugar	Horse	4 - Protecting Everleigh
Nancy Hoch	Stackable Reads	Bookstore in Glen Hollow	4 - Protecting Everleigh
Nancy Kehl	Queenie	Horse	4 - Protecting Everleigh
Nicky Ortiz	Picket Fence Realty	Real Estate Agency	4 - Protecting Everleigh
Nicky Ortiz	Homeland Guest House	Hotel in Glen Hollow	4 - Protecting Everleigh
Pam James	Miss Penny Mae	Horse	4 - Protecting Everleigh
Stacy Hartley	Marina Hayes	Everleigh's sister	4 - Protecting Everleigh
Stacy Hartley	Jazzy	Horse	4 - Protecting Everleigh
Tami Czenkus	Stella Delany	Henry's sister	4 - Protecting Everleigh
Terra Denning	Perry DeWitt	Farmer Henry purchased his house from	4 - Protecting Everleigh
Wendy Simek	Carson Simek	Town Board President	4 - Protecting Everleigh

ALSO BY PJ FIALA

You can find all of my books at https://pjfiala.com/books

Romantic Suspense

Rolling Thunder Series

Moving to Love, Book 1

Moving to Hope, Book 2

Moving to Forever, Book 3

Moving to Desire, Book 4

Moving to You, Book 5

Moving On, Book 6

Rolling Thunder Boxset 1, Books 1-3

Rolling Thunder Boxset 2, Books 4-6

Military Romantic Suspense

Second Chances Series

Designing Samantha's Love, Book 1

Securing Kiera's Love, Book 2

Bluegrass Security Series

Heart Thief, Book One

Finish Line, Book Two

Lethal Love, Book Three

Wrenched Fate, Book Four

Lynyrd Station Protectors - Security

Finding His Fire Book One

Finding His Mark Book Two

Finding His Jewel Book Three

Finding His Match Book Four

Big 3 Security Boxset, Books 1-3

Lynyrd Station Protectors - Special Ops

Defending Keirnan, LSP Special Ops Book One

Defending Sophie, LSP Special Ops Book Two

Defending Roxanne, LSP Special Ops Book Three

Defending Yvette, LSP Special Ops BookFour

Defending Bridget, LSP Special Ops Book Five

Defending Isabella, LSP Special Ops Book Six

LSP Special Ops Box Set One (Books 1-3)

LSP Special Ops Box Set Two (Books 4-6)

Lynyrd Station Protectors - Trafficking

RAPTOR Rising - Prequel

Saving Shelby, LSP Trafficking Book One

Holding Hadleigh, LSP Trafficking Book Two

Craving Charlesia, LSP Trafficking Book Three

Promising Piper, LSP Trafficking Book Four

Missing Mia, LSP Trafficking Book Five

Believing Becca, LSP Trafficking Book Six

Keeping Kori, LSP Trafficking Book Seven

Healing Hope, LSP Trafficking Book Eight

Engaging Emersyn, LSP Trafficking Book Nine

LSP Trafficking Box Set 1

LSP Trafficking Box Set 2

LSP Trafficking Box Set 3

GHOST Legacy (Next generation)

Finding Lara, Book One

Saving Elena, Book Two

Rescuing Kenna, Book Three

Protecting Everleigh, Book Four

Guarding Adelaide, Book Five

Shielding Maya, Book Six

Blossom Springs Series

Servicemen of Blossom Springs

Steamy Nights

Sultry Nights

Seductive Nights

MEET PJ

Writing has been a desire my whole life. Once I found the courage to write, life changed for me in the most profound way. Bringing stories to readers that I'd enjoy reading and creating characters that are flawed, but lovable is such a joy.

When not writing, I'm with my family doing something fun. My husband, Gene, and I are bikers and enjoy riding to new locations, meeting new people and generally enjoying this fabulous country we live in.

I come from a family of veterans. My grandfather, father, brother, two sons, and one daughter-in-law are all veterans. Needless to say, I am proud to be an American and proud of the service my amazing family has given.

My online home is https://www.pjfiala.com.
You can connect with me on
Facebook: https://www.facebook.com/PJFialaAuthor
Instagram: https://www.Instagram.com/PJFiala.
YouTube: https://youtube.com/@PJFiala
TikTok: https://www.tiktok.com/@pjfiala?lang=en
If you prefer to email, go ahead, I'll respond - pjfiala@ pjfiala.com.

COPYRIGHT

Copyright © 2023 by PJ Fiala

All rights reserved. This book or any portion thereof may not be reproduced or used in any manner whatsoever without the express written permission of the publisher except for the use of brief quotations in a book review.

Publisher's note: This is a work of fiction. Names, characters, places, and incidents either are the product of the author's imagination or are used fictitiously. Any resemblance to actual events, locales, or persons, living or dead, is entirely coincidental.

Printed in the United States of America

First published 2023

Fiala, PJ

GUARDING ADELAIDE / PJ Fiala

p. cm.

1. Romance—Fiction. 2. Romance—Suspense. 3. Romance - Military

I. Title – GUARDING ADELAIDE

ISBN-13: 978-1-959386-64-3

www.ingramcontent.com/pod-product-compliance
Lightning Source LLC
Chambersburg PA
CBHW072047190726
48294CB00005B/1439